THE RAWHIDERS

It was a fence that started the threat of war, as so many other wars had begun on the range that had once been free and open. This time it was worse, because it was Marti's fence ... and she was a beautiful woman who brought out the best and worst of men. This time the men got together with revenge on their minds, grabbed their guns and set out to cut the wire. Since Marshal Brandon Parker loved Marti, he had no choice but to take her side, so he quit his job as peace officer. Nothing would stop him from protecting Marti...

THE RAWHIDERS

THE RAWHIDERS

by

Lauran Paine

The Golden West Large Print Books
Long Preston, North Yorkshire,
BD23 4ND, England.

British Library Cataloguing in Publication Data.

Paine, Lauran
        The rawhiders.

        A catalogue record of this book is
        available from the British Library

        ISBN   978-1-84262-908-6 pbk

First published 1957

Published in Large Print 2013 by arrangement with
Golden West Literary Agency

The Golden West Large Print is an imprint of Library Magna
Books Ltd.

Printed and bound in Great Britain by
T.J. (International) Ltd., Cornwall, PL28 8RW

Chapter One

Brandon Parker, the level-eyed, uncomplicated Town Marshal with a pleasant look,
lean body and square jaw, stood in the sun
holding the one-piece reins to a drowsy
sorrel mare. After moments of patient
immobility the sun began to broil his brains
and the sweat ran under his shirt. He looked
up and down the roadway with an annoyed
expression, didn't see what he was looking
for and turned an unfriendly glance upon
the mare. The beast was studying him from
beneath heavy eyelids in a mocking way. He
shifted his feet, settled into a new position
and his spurs rang. He glowered at the town.

There wasn't much to see. Two sides of a
dusty road with stores facing one another. A
bank, saloon, harness shop, Nolan's Mer-
cantile – 'Best In The West' – land office, a
few other buildings and dust with heat.
That's about all there was to Fort Parker,
Arizona territory. His grandfather had
founded the place. Brandon had wondered
a thousand times – why?

Beyond the town was cow-country. An
immense slice of emptiness with grass and
trees growing on it, and scattered like seeds

cast from a gigantic hand were ranches, here and there. Big ranches, lots of cattle, riders, horses, people who lived well in the good years and just about as well in the lean years. Fort Parker country.

The sun went right on working; Brandon shifted position again. It was hotter than blue-blazes. He looked at the skimpy reins in his hand and at a nearby hitchrack without an extra inch on it where he might tie the sorrel mare. Saturday; everybody and his brother was in town.

He shook sweat off his chin. People passing behind him under the plankwalks overhang, looked. Standing out in the mid-June sun holding a horse's reins five feet from shade... Brandon squirmed. Nobody but a greenhorn would ride one-piece reins anyway; little dinky things, too short to tie by, too awkward to hold. He reached up and tilted his hat forward so the sun couldn't scratch his eyeballs.

Standing there minding his own business after lunch in the Drover's and up comes this smidgin of a girl looking like a bump on a tree on that big old mare. She had hopped down and her face brightened when she'd seen Brandon standing there in the shade. She had turned on a smile as big as all outdoors and pushed that silly one-piece rein into his hand and had then disappeared among the shoppers behind him, under the overhang.

How long ago? He squinted at the sun from beneath his hatbrim; must have been half an hour ago. Brandon scowled darkly, pulled himself upright and flashed a long look up and down the roadway, both sides. No sign of her. If there was a place to tie the tomfool critter...

'Hello.'

He started, swung and looked down. She didn't quite come up to his shoulder. Her eyes were as blue as cornflowers. He noticed something that had escaped him before; freckles. A little sifting of them over the saddle of her nose. Not very many and golden rather than tan. Her mouth was curled up into a guileless smile; a very pretty mouth with white teeth. She raised up a little on her toes and pushed a bundle into his free arm.

'Would you?' she said with that sweeter-than-sweet smile. 'For just a second longer?'

He watched her whip around and hurry down the plankwalk again. She wasn't very tall he thought, but what there was of her was just enough. Not too much and not too little. Her hair was like washed gold, the way the sun skidded off it. Golly; she was pretty as a picture. The bundle in his arms moved. He almost dropped it in astonishment. It moved again. With quickening misgiving he looked down at it. A baby!

Brandon began to perspire anew. Holding the hip-shot sorrel mare who was regarding him with unblinking interest, with one hand, the baby with the other, the sun was worrying away at him, he was completely and totally uncomfortable.

A frightening thought occurred to him. What if she didn't come back? Had an accident or forgot him? He wrestled with panic, got it under control but felt the back of his neck burning red. A tall tawny cowboy was standing two feet away, looking at him. There was no amusement in the newcomer's face, just a thoughtful, rather speculative appraisal.

'Howdy, Charley,' Brandon said, the back of his neck getting redder.

Charley moved a little closer, still with no definable expression. He leaned a little and gazed down at the baby. 'Must be,' he said finally. 'Same hair, same chin,' then he straightened up and began to make a cigarette without another word or glance.

Brandon Parker said: 'Smart aleck.' He might have said more but the baby squirmed again, this time lashing out with feet the size of a child's fist, in a distressful, wrathful way. Brandon looked down, his panic returning. The baby made some unpleasant sounds. Brandon hoisted his arm a little to change the infant's position. Charley lit his cigarette and watched, smoke trailing up from his nose. Several passers-by turned to look. The baby let out a peal of anger. Brandon, scarlet started to raise the hand with the one-piece reins. When the line tightened the big mare roused herself, threw back her head, snorted and pulled back. Brandon fought for balance and had to let the rein go. Charley moved swiftly, caught the mare as she started to move. When he stepped back onto the plank-walk holding the rein loosely in one hand he cocked a glance at Brandon.

'Halter-puller. Now I see why you didn't tie her up.'

Brandon said nothing. He was jouncing the baby with both hands trying to quell its squalling fury. Tiny red fists beat the air impotently. Brandon gathered up the blanket and looped it swath-like around the strug-gling, cry-yelling little body. He snuggled the child against his chest. It arched its back against him, aroused to new heights of red-faced fury.

Charley looking on, said: 'Well; don't strangle it, Brandy. It's got to breathe.'

'Mind your own business!' Brandon said in a breathless way, thoroughly absorbed in his battle with the squirming yelling infant.

Charley shrugged, smoke going up one side of his face. 'Sure,' he said easily. 'Here, take your mare, too.' He held out the reins.

Brandon looked at him in a helpless, frus-trated way and said nothing. Made no move to take the rein. People were stopping,

11

peering out at them both from under the overhang. The baby was in full cry, its face screwed up into an unbelievably ugly little tight, red knot, all lines and anger. Charley's detached calmness was an anchor in the terrible embarrassment and helplessness. Brandon tried to reach it. 'Isn't mine,' he said between struggles with the baby. 'Thing's got more legs'n a centipede.'

Charley looked up. 'Isn't it?' he said. 'How'd you get it; raffle?'

A big-bosomed elderly woman came close. Charley obliging stepped back. She bent her head, peered at the baby, then drew far back and fired a glare at Brandon. 'Ought to be horsewhipped,' she said fiercely. 'Modern parents! Out here in the sun.' She made a short, imperative gesture. 'Get back there in the shade.'

Brandon moved back as though retreating. The elderly woman stomped along in front of him. She had a downy mustache, bear-trap mouth, and kindling little eyes. 'Now, you bring that baby along.' She didn't wait to see if Brandon was following, just turned and in a flat-footed way stumped into the Drover's Saloon. Brandon trailed after her.

It was wonderfully cool inside the Drover's. There was a musky man-smell in there. The woman went straight up to the bar and thumped it with a purse as big as a saddlebag. Frosty Turner, the barkeep, came up like a man in a trance.

'Yes'm?'

'Milk!'

Frosty looked over the woman's head at Brandon at the contorting bundle that emitted snarling sounds in a tremulous key, and back to the woman again.

'MILK! YOU DOLT!'

Frosty jumped. 'Milk,' he repeated. 'Ma'm; this is a saloon. We don't handle milk in here.' He said it like he was ashamed of himself.

'You get some milk and you get it right now. Do you want a sick baby on your conscience?'

Frosty shot Brandon a venomous look and walked stiffly toward the kitchen-annex where they cooked meals for the Drover's Café.

Brandon was watching Frosty when the baby almost flung itself out of his arms. He caught his breath and clamped down. The woman made a strangling sound of her own and snatched the baby away from him. She laid it upon the bartop and spoke aside to Brandon.

'Get one of those clean bar rags over there. No, you simpleton – there – over there hanging on that spike.'

Brandon got the bar rag and watched. The woman's hands sped like magic. When she was finished the baby seemed to quiet down

13

a little. Frosty came back with a little pan that had warm milk in it. The woman plumped the wet diaper down on the bar and Frosty winced.

'Give me another of those rags.'

Brandon reached for the rag the same time Frosty did. Their faces were inches apart. Frosty's voice, low and vehement, went no further than Brandon's ear. He used one savage word to impugn Brandon's legitimacy then turned with the rag and handed it, poker-faced, to the woman. She handily twisted one end of it, soaked it in the milk and gave it to the baby. Instantly the infant relaxed all over and began to suck the rag. The woman watched for a moment then heaved a big sigh. Frosty watched impassively. His glance flicked to the soggy diaper on the bartop. His lips tightened. He lifted the thing with two fingers and dropped it into a waste bucket behind him. Brandon, sun-baked, dehydrated, looked longingly at some sparkling ale mugs on the backbar shelf. He ran his tongue over his lips.

'Frosty?'

'No!'

The elderly woman turned at the sound of Brandon's voice like a blind rattler. 'Young man,' she said, taking a firm grip on the big wide strap of her over-sized purse. 'Where is your wife?'

Frosty said: 'He doesn't have one, ma'm.

He's the Town Marshal.'

The woman's angry little eyes seemed to congeal like freezing water. 'Ahhhh!' she said. The sound reminded Brandon of something awfully unpleasant. 'One of *those*, are you; well, you look the part.' The woman ran her eyes over Brandon's lean length, his holstered gun, his carelessly worn hat. 'You look the part. Made her give it up, did you?' She didn't let him answer. 'You'd *do* that, wouldn't you!' A big vein in the woman's neck began to swell. She clutched the strap of her purse meaningly. 'I've got a notion to give you what-for. I've heard of men like you, you – you...!'

Helplessly Brandon said: 'Frosty?'

The barman refused to lift his eyes. With one hand he stroked his handlebar mustache while he gazed pensively at the baby. It was rolling its eyes at him. Frosty's mouth lifted a little at the corners, in spite of him. He reached down, took the rag, dipped it into the milk and gave it back to the baby, who immediately wreathed its face in a beatific smile.

'Frosty?'

'Shuttup!'

The woman was sucking in a big gulp of air when Brandon heard spurred boots approaching from the rear. He made himself turn. It was Charley Belton.

'Charley; tell her – it isn't mine.'

Charley looked mildly at the three of them when he answered. 'Isn't it?' He paused a second. 'I just came in to tell you I gave the horse to a kid to hold. I'm going to ride over and look at the Grant fence.'

'Wait,' Brandon said, quickly. 'I'll–'

'Oh no you don't,' Frosty said without moving anything but his eyes. 'You don't run off and leave it in here, Brandy.'

'Abandon your own child, would you?' the big woman said, lifting the purse like a club. 'I'll teach you – you philandering young–'

'Hello. The little boy holding my horse said you were in here.'

Brandon recognized the voice. He looked down at her. The same stirring smile. The same mobile mouth curled up, the spun-gold hair and the golden freckles. She was looking up at him in her guileless way. Big blue eyes. He was vaguely conscious of a strange emotion struggling to life behind his belt-buckle somewhere. Not too much, not too little, just enough.

The blue eyes swept from his face to the bartop. 'Ohhh,' she said in her musical way. 'You're wonderful; knew just what he wanted, didn't you? He's happy, isn't he?'

The elderly woman's face pinched down with disapproval. 'Young lady,' she said, ominously. 'You ought to be–'

The blue eyes swept over the craggy face, mustached upper lip and all when she said:

16

'I knew someone like you would come along if he got into trouble.' She looked up at Charley for the first time. His narrowed eyes were watching her, from an expressionless face; there was a hint of a twinkle in them. 'I like this country,' the girl said. 'It really has wonderful people in it – hasn't it?'

No one answered her. She went closer to the bar reached for the baby, lifted it, snuggled it gently and laid a small hand on the older woman's arm. 'You're wonderful,' the musical voice said. It was as though a burnished shaft of sunlight had come into the darkest recess old the old bar-room.

The big woman's fingers relaxed on the purse strap. 'Well,' she said, 'seems like you young parents got to be told now and again. Out in the sun and all – I raised seven...'

'I wish I had someone like you to – well – you know: to talk to.' There was a soft echo after the girl's words.

Brandon met Frosty's glance over the top of her head. The barman looked enthralled. Charley was blank-faced as usual, just looking. The twinkle was gone from his eyes. In its place was a peculiar warmth. He dropped his cigarette and stomped it, raised his head as the girl, yawning baby in her arms, went past flashing her heart-melting smile. 'Thank you ever so much – all of you.' Charley nodded slightly, the warmth glowing in his face, but the girl's gaze rested longest on Brandon;

seemed to kindle a little. 'Real Westerners,' she murmured, then she was gone.

In the saloon it was as though the sun had gone behind a cloud. An awkward moment of deep silence fell. Charley, gazing at Brandon's face, said: 'Well; we've wasted enough time, but we can still get out there and see that fence.'

Brandon nodded without speaking and the elderly woman shot him a puzzled look, grunted and went around them toward the door. Frosty pushed up off the counter, gazed at it a moment where the baby had been, then shrugged and made an automatic swipe with his bar rag.

Charley looked impatient. 'Well?' he said.

They left the Drover's, crossed the roadway, got their horses from the lean-to behind the Marshal's office, swung up and rode westerly beyond town.

For a long time Brandon didn't speak. He had an idiosyncrasy of silence. It didn't mean anything in particular; just that he was absorbed with some thought, some idea. Charley didn't push him until, an hour and a half later, they topped a landswell and reined up. Below and northward was a fence. The sunshine sprang off the taut barbed-wire like it was white-hot. Fence posts, new enough to look raw, marched in a painfully straight line to the farthest dip in the horizon.

Charley put both hands on the horn and

leaned a little. 'Seven miles of it,' he said, squinting. 'Must have cost a fortune. Cuts the range straight in half.' He bobbed his head at the fence. 'Not a gate in it anywhere.'

Brandon looked and the reflected light hurt his eyes. 'Who put it up?'

'Grant ranch; you know that.'

'No; I mean the man. Grant died last year. Who took over?'

Charley's gaze drifted to the broad sweep of range beyond the fence. On the far side the grass was six inches taller than the feed on the near side.

'Darned if I know,' he said. 'Heirs. I heard around town they're greenhorns. Easterners.'

Brandon also noticed the difference in the feed. His stockman's soul recognized the merit of the fence. His cattleman's free-range heritage was antagonized by the shimmering wire, the army of posts. Without much conviction he said, 'Well; I suppose they've got a right to fence in their own land.'

'The right,' Charley said, emphasizing the last word. 'It's deeded land, sure.' He lapsed into silence long enough to make a cigarette, light it and exhale. In an altogether different tone he said: 'They'll cut that fence in so many places it'll look like a busted spool of thread.'

A battered wagon lurched up out of a swale across the fence. There were three men in it, cowboys from the looks of them.

They saw the two riders on the hill and the wagon stopped.

Charley made a little grin. 'Act like they've been caught stealing apples,' he said.

The three men in the wagon were motionless, gazing up at them. Brandon lifted his reins. 'Let's go down.'

They picked their way slowly toward the wagon. Closer, fence wire danced in the brilliant sunlight. Both riders screwed up their eyes against the glare. Brandon swung down and tossed his tie-rope over a post. He waved casually at the men in the wagon. One of them called out something to the team, the wagon creaked closer. Charley Belton got down and stood loosely, holding his split-reins, waiting.

'Howdy.'

Brandon looked at the men. Two were young and clean-shaven, the third man was older, leathery-visaged, tough as all outdoors. Near the older one's hand, leaning carelessly, was the snout of a Winchester carbine. None of the three looked exactly friendly nor at ease.

Brandon ran his sleeve under his chin to mop off sweat as he spoke. 'You fellers building this fence?'

The older man with dead-faded eyes that never blinked nor batted said: 'Yeah.' He said it sharply, a little defiantly.

'Lot of work,' Brandon said, looking down

the row of posts.

The older man relaxed. His hand, holding the sideboard near the carbine, relaxed. 'You got no idea,' he said warmly. 'Man – it's nothin' *but* work. Damn' posts twenty-five feet apart no matter what? Hit rock you dassent move over five feet, they got to be right on the twenty-five foot line.' He looked distastefully at the taut strands of wire separating the wagoneers from the horsemen. 'And that stuff'll eat you alive. Whips around like a blind snake.' He wagged his head at the fence.

The younger men up on the wagon-seat didn't speak. They were both eyeing Brandon and Charley out of eyes the color of dirty silver, faded and dry looking from sunglare. Neither of them seemed relaxed with the horsemen. One of them had nostrils that twitched. It made Charley Belton think of a wolf testing the air for scent.

'Whose building it?' Brandon went on.

'Grant ranch,' the older man said.

'Yeah,' Charley said dryly. 'We figured that much. Who's on the Grant place now? Old Beasely kicked off last year.'

'Oh. You mean who're the new owners. Folks from back East name of Grant. Youngsters. Kinsfolk of the old man.'

Brandon considered this a moment before he spoke again. 'Are they home now, do you reckon?'

'Well,' the older man said thoughtfully, 'they was this morning when we lit out, but I think the lady said she had to go to town last night at supper. We leave pretty early with the wagon though,' the man said, then he waved an arm that had a snagged and torn sleeve on it. 'Ride down there three miles and you'll come to a place we ain't finished yet. You can ride right across through the fence. Ranch is northwest from there.'

Brandon thanked them. He and Charley rode away at a walk. Once, from a landswell's ridge, Charley twisted and looked back. The men in the wagon hadn't moved. Charley cleared his throat and spat.

'Hard-working crew,' he said. Then: 'Ride three miles to a hole in the fence.' He sounded disgusted.

Knowing the trend of Charley's thoughts Brandon remained neutral. 'It's their land.'

'Aw hell,' Charley said. 'If you had a calf under that fence and his mammy on this side would you ride maybe three miles to get around the fence to drive him out? You know you wouldn't and neither would I.'

'Yes you would,' Brandon said. 'We both would. It's their land. They've got a right to fence it if they want to.'

'You might, Brandy; the cowmen won't. They'll cut it.'

'They better never get caught doing that.'

'Who's going to catch them? Even if Grant

riders saw them doing it they'd have to ride maybe five miles around their own fence to go after them. It's silly.'

'They've still got the right, though.'

'Bull,' Charley said with feeling. 'They're just asking for trouble is all, and they'll get it. Most of the outfits we've been turning out here for fifty years. You hang a necklace of wire like this right smack-dab down the middle of *anyone's* range and you'll make more enemies than you can shake a stick at.'

'You, too?'

Charley looked over at Brandon. 'I'm talking about all the big outfits, Brandy. The Spanners, Old Man Fortin, Wagonwheel, the Bow outfit. All of 'em. I'm only a little feller. Bad enough to have greenhorns running stock on the range without them bucking all the big outfits too.'

Brandon saw the unfinished part of the fence and headed through it. Charley followed him. Immediately their horses were trailing through pastern-high feed. Dry, of course, because it was the middle of summer, but good dry-feed. The kind that would keep a wet-cow making plenty of milk.

'See the difference, Charley?'

Belton didn't reply. He rode with his glance fixed on the lip of land far ahead, beyond which lay the Grant ranch buildings. Down in an emerald meadow where Cottonwood Creek meandered. Without looking at his companion he spoke, finally.

'It'll hurt me a little but not as much as it'll hurt Bow and the Spanners. I'm not big enough. Three hundred cows isn't much of a herd.'

Brandon watched the prairie drop off ahead; slope downward toward the buildings which were just beginning to appear over the edge of the horizon.

'Charley – do you think the range'll ever change?'

'What do you mean, "ever". It's changed right now. That fence changed it.'

'All right. Didn't you ever think this might happen; someone might start ranching scientifically? Fence in, control their breeding, make better beef on better feed?'

'You've been reading a book,' Charley said.

'Answer me.'

Charley made a motion with his hand. 'You're thinking about it wrong, Brandy. The thing is – this is a big country. There's plenty of room for all of us. Why hog any of it?'

Brandon looked thoughtfully, meaningly, at the tall grass underfoot. 'It isn't this tall on the other side of the fence,' he said. 'And if the country's big enough, why then, what these people fence in shouldn't hurt too much.'

'Oh for Chrissake,' Charley exploded. 'Don't give me that.'

'Well, look at the feed, Charley. This is

what the whole country'll come to some day. You'll fence, too.'

'Pig's eye,' Charley said sharply.

'Yes you will. You'll have to. Listen; if Grant ranch turns out better finished critters at shipping time they'll get the best price. The rest of you'll take the leavings. They can do it by saving their grass, by giving the ranch a chance to reseed itself, by not over-grazing.'

'Over-grazing, hell,' Belton said, reining his horse over into the wagon rut that dipped down toward the Grant ranch buildings. 'You can't overstock twenty-eight thousand acres of land.'

'Oh yes you can.'

A man draping team-harnesses over a corral looked up as they rode into the yard. He said 'Howdy.' Charley Belton shot him a dark look and grunted. The man's smile faded a little. Brandon said 'Howdy,' reining over toward the house. The man by the hanging harness watched them ride past, spat an amber stream and ambled toward a log bunkhouse.

Brandon pulled up before the house. Across the veranda between the uprights was stretched a rope. Upon it hung yards of square wet-wash that nearly hid the front of the house. Brandon swung down, dropped his tie-rope over a rail and waited for Charley. Belton walked around his horse's rear toward the house with his gaze going over the laundry distastefully. He and Brandon had known old Beasely Grant, who would have turned over in his grave if he could have seen all that stuff draped across the front of his house. Old Beasely Grant had been like iron. He sparked when rubbed.

Brandon, up ahead, was almost to the steps when Charley's head snapped back, his eyes leapt to the laundry, noted its squareness, its repetitive sameness, and comprehension struck him like a blow. Brandon didn't look up again until he was on the veranda and a masculine voice said:

'Mornin'. Can I help you?'

Brandon smiled. He was looking at a boy not over eighteen, but as tall as Brandon was. The features were vaguely, disturbingly familiar. A new shell-belt and holster encircled the lean waist of the youth and his eyes, agate blue, never wavered. There was something about the face – something pantherish, unnatural...

'My name's Brandon Parker. Marshal at Fort Parker. This is Charley Belton, sort of a neighbor of yours to the northeast. Thought we'd ride over and – and–'

'Hello.'

Her eyes were dancing at him from a freshly scrubbed and shiny face. She was standing so erectly, framed in the old doorway, that Brandon had to fight to keep his eyes steady, the surprise from showing.

'Come in. I just made a fresh pot of coffee.'

He didn't speak until they were inside. Charley's face was blank, his eyes taking in the leashed-violence look of the tall boy, the way the girl deftly swept aside some ironing on the big kitchen table.

She spoke while she moved. Brandon followed every turn, every curve. Her hair was all swept back and had a green ribbon holding it in a pony-tail that bobbed and swayed when she laid out the big cups and poured them full.

'Sit down. Oh golly – excuse me. This is my brother Milton. Milt, this is – is...'

'Yes, I know,' the boy said carelessly. 'The Town Marshal and his running-mate.'

Charley, in the act of drawing a chair under him, stopped. His eyes went to the boy's face and stayed there. 'My name's Belton,' he said. 'Charley Belton.'

The boy nodded, returning Charley's look. 'Sure,' he said. 'You've got a woodtick pasture east of us.'

Charley went down into the chair slowly, his eyes staying on the boy's face. He didn't speak though, and finally turned, snugged the cup of coffee closer and peered down into it.

'Sugar there, gentlemen. Here's cream.'

Brandon shoved his legs far under the table and looked at her. 'Mind if I ask your name?' he said.

Her blue eyes across the table from him, raised. 'No, it's Grant. Marti Grant. My brother is Milton Grant.'

'Oh.' Brandon touched the coffee to his lips. It almost scalded him. 'Is your husband at home, Mrs Grant?'

The boy laughed. It sounded to Charley like some one dropping bullets on a piece of glass. 'She's got no husband. Never been married, me either.'

'My,' Charley said mildly. 'I was sure *you'd* been married.'

Milton's face got red, his eyes flashed at Charley.

Remembering the baby, Brandon was stunned. He drank coffee to cover it up, set the cup down and looked over at her. 'Uh – do you own the ranch now?'

'Yes. Uncle Beasely left it to us. We're from Indiana, originally.'

Charley, still locking horns with Milton, said: 'Indiana. Do they carry guns back there, sonny?'

Milton saw red. His jaw muscles rippled. Hate of a strange and violent kind showed in his glare. He wouldn't answer, but his sister did.

'No. You see, we're from a city. Indianapolis, it's called.'

Brandon was drawing imprints of cattle brands on the oilcloth with the tip of a spoon. 'Who is your foreman, ma'm?' he asked without looking up.

Her lips curled. The glance she gave him was warm, trusting. 'Milton is – but we have five riders. One used to work for my uncle. They guide us a lot.' She shot a quick glance at Milton, whose color was still high, his eyes hard and unfriendly, fixed on big Charley Belton, who was stirring his coffee as though trying to see if there was a bottom to the cup, and not looking at any of them.

Brandon was stumped. He shifted a little on the chair.

'More coffee, Sheriff?'

'Town Marshal. No thanks; maybe Charley–'

'Believe not, thanks,' Charley said, still stirring thoughtfully.

'Too strong?' Milton asked acidly.

Charley laid aside the spoon with the air of a man embarking upon some unpleasantness he only half regretted. 'Won't float a horseshoe,' he said, gazing fixedly at Milton. 'Was that fence your idea, sonny?'

Milton's knuckles were white in his lap. 'And if it was?' he countered.

Brandon looked swiftly from one of them to the other and pulled himself up straighter in the chair. 'Uh – Milton, don't get riled.'

'Who's gettin' riled?'

'Nobody, I hope,' Brandon said quickly, levering up a smile of sorts. 'We're just interested in the thing. You see, there's never been a fence in the Fort Parker country before.'

Marti Grant spoke. 'It was my idea, gentlemen. I thought the grass might do better if animals were kept off it part of the year.' She said it in the same tone she'd used to the big woman in the Drover's Saloon and Brandon felt himself relaxing. He gazed at her across the table. Pretty as a picture, even with a shiny nose. That funny feeling behind his belt-buckle came to life again. Groping for something to say he asked how the baby was and as soon as he'd said it he turned brick-red. Sweat ran under his shirt.

'He's fine. Would you like to see him?' The words were warm, vibrant.

Brandon nodded because it was the easiest thing to do, but he didn't want to see the baby. She arose with quick, sure movements. The sun broke over her hair when she moved past the window. Charley was looking at him strangely; he knew it without looking around.

'Here he is. There.' She placed the warm bundle in Brandon's arms. He held it instinctively, breathing very shallowly and hoping it was asleep. She sat across from him again, the blue of her eyes shades darker. 'We haven't named him yet. Milton isn't very good with names.' The blue gaze burst over Brandon's face with abrupt inspiration. 'What would *you* name him?'

Charley Belton made a loud noise in his

coffee cup.

'I wouldn't begin to know how to name it – him,' Brandon said miserably. He was suffering. The room seemed to be moving in around him. The air was close, stifling hot. He looked at Milton. The youth's eyes were steely with a steady flow of animosity. Not sullenness; just plain dislike. 'Uh – what names did you suggest, Milton?'

'I said name him after his paw.'

Brandon's heart misfired and thudded against his ribs with a sharp stab of pain. He nodded weakly. The damned idiot was going to bring it out in the open. Brandon could see it on his face and he couldn't think of a single thing to say to head it off.

'His name was Jack Porter. He worked for our folks back East. He and his wife died in the 'flu epidemic. Marti had to have the kid.' He looked at his sister and back to Brandon. 'Women're like that.'

'You like him and you know it,' his sister said.

'Oh, sure,' the boy said carelessly. 'But he'll be a long time getting big enough to do much, is all.'

Charley was gazing at Marti. 'Didn't it have any kinsfolk back East?'

'No. The Porters said they were alone. They asked us to keep him.'

Charley nodded his head up and down, flicked his fingernails across the table-top

31

making a little drumming sound.

'He's asleep,' Milton said.

Brandon looked down. The baby had tiny beads of perspiration on its upper lip. One fist no larger than a prune was close to its mouth. It *was* kind of pretty.

'Here. I'll put him back to bed.'

She took him. Close like that, Brandon could see the way her eyelashes were; long and oddly dark for one of her coloring, and up-curling. When she left the room he faced toward her brother. 'Milton, where are you going to put gates in that fence?'

'Aren't,' Milton said shortly.

Charley was still drumming on the table. Brandon gazed across from him at the lean willow of a youth. 'You should,' he said. 'Suppose someone else's critter gets through it. How's the owner going to get it out?'

'Come to the ranch and tell us. We'll run it out.'

'Run it five miles along the fence to the main gate?' Brandon shook his head. 'Milton, did you ever try to drive a scairt calf all by itself? It just about can't be done.'

'How would it get through the fence anyway, unless someone put it through?'

Brandon was looking at a height of ignorance he'd never run across before. Born and raised in cow-country it seemed incredible that anyone would ask a question like that. Very patiently he said: 'It happens right along, Milton. A calf kneels down to reach under the bottom wire for the tall grass on the other side. Pretty soon he's pushing a little. Next thing you know he's bawling like the devil and his mammy's on the other side running up and down.'

Charley said quietly: 'Like squeezing a seed out of a grape. That's what they look like when they're breaching.'

'Breaching?'

'Going under a fence – or through it.'

Marti came back and poured them all more coffee. Brandon stole another look at her eyelashes. She was looking at him from beneath them and he turned red all over. She said, 'Sugar?' as though she hadn't noticed anything and he took it, spooned in a smidgin and hated himself for doing it because he detested coffee with sugar in it. She sat down again.

Milton took out the makings and began to labor over a cigarette. Charley watched him and when the boy was half finished Charley took up the sack and papers, rolled a one-handed cigarette, popped it carelessly into his mouth and flicked a match waiting for Milton to finish. After they'd both exhaled Charley broke the match and lay it beside his cup.

'There's never been a partition fence like you're building in this country. We've all used the range and worked together, sort of, at roundup time. That fence'll cut off at least three big ranches from feed they've been using for fifty years.'

Milton leaned far back in his chair watching Charley and smoking. 'You don't think they'll like it?' he asked.

Charley's cigarette emitted a quick burst of smoke, otherwise his expression didn't change. 'Think? I *know* they won't like it. Bad enough to fence folks away from their feed, but when you won't put in any gates that's like hitting them from behind.'

'But it's our land,' Marti said, looking straight at Charley.

He returned her look but his voice dropped a notch. 'Ma'm, if I owned the yard around this house and fenced it so's you couldn't get inside – would you feel friendly about it?'

'She doesn't have to feel friendly about it,' Milton said flatly.

Charley's drumming fingers stopped in mid-air. A tiny muscle in the side of his face twitched. His eyes left Marti's face and stopped on the wall between the two Grants.

The girl spoke. 'But it is improving the range, Mr Belton.'

'Not outside the fence, ma'm,' Charley said gravely.

'We don't care about the outside. We own the inside,' Milton said.

Charley stooped, picked up his hat and stood up. He didn't look at the youth. 'Thanks for the coffee, ma'm.' He twirled the hat with his fingers, looking down at her.

Brandon arose, too. She stood up then. 'It isn't very fair, is it, Sheriff?'

'Marshal, ma'm.'

'Is it?'

Brandon groped for an answer, conscious of their eyes, especially Charley Belton's. 'There're two sides to it all right,' he said.

Milton got to his feet. 'Yeah. Our side of the fence and their side. They stay out and we'll stay in. It's our land and feed. The law's on our side – if they make trouble.'

Brandon looked reprovingly at Milton without answering. Marti moved. He caught the spun-gold reflection of hair. 'Thanks for the coffee,' he said. 'It hit the spot.'

He left the ranch feeling wholly inadequate. A protective sense was troubling him. She was so little, pretty, and so – so...

'Brandy; just which side are you on, anyway?'

They were riding back toward the hole in the fence when Charley asked that. A long way off, on Brandon's right, came the squeaking, complaining sounds of the wagon. Birds flew out of the grass at their feet and a few fat cattle watched them go by.

'The law's side, Charley, I guess you'd say.'

'Quit beatin' around the bush.'

'There're two sides to it and you're not trying to see their side at all, Charley.'

'I see it plenty plain. They've got a deed to

the land so they can fence it in. That cuts everyone else out whether they've used that land for fifty years or not – me included.'

'You said it wouldn't hurt you much.'

'It won't, but I'm in the cow business. If I ever want to grow bigger I can't. She's got me blocked off the range and that squirt of a kid, that brother of hers – I could have back-handed him across the room. Smart aleck punk. Wish I'd taken that gun and–'

'Got nothing to do with it,' Brandon said suddenly.

'You'll think it has the first time he pops off to a Wagonwheel rider or the Spanner boys or old Jared Hoxey, like he did to us. They'll slit his ears and yank his arms through 'em; you'll see.'

They rode all the way back to Fort Parker in silence. When Brandon dismounted beside the lean-to behind his office where he kept his horses, Charley Belton stayed in his saddle. The sun was hot enough to scald water.

'Got to be heading back, Brandy; got chores to do.'

'Well,' Brandon said. 'I don't know what to tell you, Charley. It's their land, their fence. They've got a right to build the thing.'

'You said that before.' Charley seemed to be thinking of something. 'Did you forget about the barbecue and dance on the Fourth?'

Brandon looked up at him blankly.

'The Fourth,' Charley said. 'Fourth of July, damn it; Independence Day. The dance.'

'Oh,' Brandon grunted it, color running into his face. 'You mean – her?'

Charley looked pained. 'I didn't mean her brother,' he said, lifting his rein hand. 'Man, you're sure thick sometimes, Brandy.'

'Well...'

'You haven't asked Jemima, I know, because I saw her in town couple days ago and she said she wasn't sure she was coming over.' Charley reined around. 'Adios, Brandy – you muttonhead.'

Brandon watched Charley ride out toward the road. He stood holding his reins for a full minute, then he off-saddled, put up his horse, forked him a flake of hay and went into his little office with the adjoining cell, which smelt of sheep-dip disinfectant and was forlornly vacant between Saturday nights. Not a smoking man, exactly, he nevertheless made a cigarette and lit it. Sat down behind the desk and cocked the chair back, propped his legs up on the desk and gazed at the far wall. Fourth of July...

'Man!'

He said it so softly it sounded miles away. But he couldn't; just plain couldn't. With Jemima Fortin it was different. He'd grown up with her. Asking Marti Grant... His palms were clammy-damp; he just couldn't.

With a sensation of deep guilt he switched his thoughts to her brother and was on surer ground. Charley had been right, of course. Anyone else would have eaten the young fool alive.

And the fence.

He leaned forward, dropped the cigarette into the spittoon, leaned back and put both hands behind his head. Lord, but she was pretty...

Chapter Two

Four days later Brandon was around in back dunging out the horse-shed when three shadows filled the doorway cutting off the light. Jim and Ed and Fat Spanner, brothers who owned and operated the Spanner.

Brandon straightened up and leaned the manure against the wall.

'Howdy, fellers.'

They said 'Howdy' and the thick-set, squat one everyone had called Fat since he'd been a kid, edged inside where it was cool. Brandon felt resigned, he knew what was coming.

'What's on your minds?'

'That fence,' Fat Spanner said. 'What are you to do about it, Brandy?'

'Nothing, I didn't build it.'

Fat's little eyes grew still. 'You're the law.'

Brandon took a big gulp of air and leaned against the manger. 'It's their land, fellers. They can grow pigs on it for all the law cares. So long as they don't start a fire that spreads or something like that, the law can't stop them from making improvements.'

'You call *that* an improvement?'

Brandy looked irritated. 'You know what I mean. If she builds fences all over her range it's no violation of the law that I know of.'

'There's range law,' Jim, the youngest Spanner, said.

Brandon glanced briefly at him. Fat was the eldest. The thinker and planner. He directed his words to Fat. 'You know better than that,' he said.

'That cuts us out of six thousand acres of feed, Brandy,' Fat said quietly. 'Fall feed.' The way he said it sounded to Brandon as though the Spanners would fight to keep that feed.

'The land belongs to her, Fat.'

For a moment no one spoke. Fat shoved off the wall. 'We could go to court,' he said.

Brandon shrugged. 'No one'll stop you, Fat, only I think you'll be wasting your money.'

'Why?'

'I just told you. She owns the land. She can raise hell out there and prop it up if she wants to. It's no one's business but her own what she does on her own ground.'

'There are other ways,' Fat said.

Brandon wasn't a swearing man, but he felt like swearing right then. 'Cut it out, Fat. You don't mean that and you know it. Those days are past.'

Fat moved back out into the dazzling sunlight. Over his shoulder he said, 'Are they?' His brothers followed him back around to the roadway and Brandon reached for his shirt, donned it, and walked in a disgruntled frame of mind out of the lean-to.

'Fence!'

He stalked into his office, tossed his hat on the desk and filled a wash-basin, scrubbed off sweat, dust and dirt, made a cigarette, something he rarely did, went over and sat behind the desk.

'Fence!'

It was shimmering hot out but it was cool inside the office. He fell asleep and didn't awaken until the cigarette burnt his fingers. With an oath he threw the thing into the brass spittoon and had his hand half-way to his face when the door opened and she stood framed in the squared piece of brassy sunlight.

'Hello.'

He got up swiftly. 'Afternoon, Miss Grant. Come in and close the door.'

She wore a dress that flared out in a billowing way from the waist down but which was snug from the waist up. There was a little black ribbon worked in and out of the high neckline. Her hair was swept up and over ears.

That funny feeling was behind his belt again.

'Is this a business call?' he said, moving up the slat-bottomed chair.

She puckered her forehead at him. 'Well – half and half.' She sat down and kept her eyes on him as he went around the desk and faced her.

She looked so cool. There was a word that described her but he couldn't find it. Pretty as a fat heifer in a clover patch. Little, with a nose that turned up just the littlest bit. A saddle of golden freckles. That direct way she looked at you. The way she was put together. There was a word...

'Sheriff.'

'No, Miss Grant, there's a difference. You see, I'm *deputy* sheriff, but only when I'm beyond town. Out the country, you see. Otherwise my regular job, the full-time one, is Town Marshal.'

'Oh.' It left the softest echo in the office, the way she said it.

Unconsciously he looked at the far wall. He'd never heard an echo in his office before.

'Marshal,' she enunciated it very clearly and hesitated a second after say it. 'Marshal – were you warning us the other day, you and Mr Belton? I mean about the fence? Did you mean other people – the cattlemen – were going to be disagreeable about it?'

'Yes,' he said. 'As a matter of fact I had callers this morning about the fence.' He couldn't see the freckles across the desk, but he knew they were there. In a hollow of her throat the faint pulse beat sturdily. He leaned upon the desk. There wasn't a flaw in her complexion.

'Uh – you see, like we told you, there's never been fence in this country. Your uncle used to run his stock on Bow and Wagon-wheel, and their stock ran on him. It was a sort of mutual business. At roundup time everyone helped everyone else. It's always been like that.'

'And now it won't be?'

'No. You've cut the range almost in half.'

'But Marshal, we don't want to run our cattle on other people and we don't want them to run their stock on us. Isn't that all right?'

Brandon said: 'It's legal. I don't know of any law you're breaking by fencing the Grant place in, ma'm. The thing is – folks never had it happen before. They can't get used to the fence or the idea of it.'

'And they don't like it.'

He said 'No,' and dropped his eyes to the desk. A calendar with a big numeral One snagged his eye. The first of July. Three more days... He cleared his throat and kept his face averted.

'Will they get used to it?' she asked. 'We don't want to start out making enemies.'

His mind flashed back to that day in the saloon, the way she'd handled the big woman, he and Charley. There was a twinkle in his eye when next he spoke.

'You've got a knack, ma'm. I don't think they'll fight you. Uh – but your brother's got a lot to learn.'

She studied his face a moment. 'He's just a boy, Marshal.'

Brandon wasn't thinking about Milton. He was thinking of the Fourth of July celebration, but it was easier to talk about her brother and the new gun he wore.

'Out here,' he said, 'men wear guns because – well – they've been raised with them. Now your brother – I don't suppose he's practiced much with a gun – and he seemed a mite quick-tempered. A man wearing a gun dassen't be hot-headed, ma'm.'

'He's young. The gun is the best thing in the world for his – his – self-confidence, Marshal. It makes him feel fully grown up. Do you see?'

'Uh-huh,' Brandon said doubtfully. 'As long as he doesn't mouth off at the wrong time that'll be fine.'

'I know he antagonized Mr Belton, but it wasn't his fault.'

'Charley?' Brandon said defensively. 'Why, Charley Belton's the nicest feller in the whole Fort Parker country. He wouldn't take Milton down a notch. Charley's wool and a yard wide.'

'Understanding?'

'More understanding than anyone I know, but there are some fellers around the country that aren't. It's what I meant when I said Milton ought to go slow.' He was thinking of the Spanner brothers.

'It's too bad, isn't it?' She said it pensively, looking straight into his eyes.

'What's too bad; Milton's gun?'

'All this – over a fence.'

He blinked at her. Seven miles of three-strand barbed-wire fence wasn't anything trivial. Neither was the feeling he couldn't define, but which grew inside him whenever she was around.

'Ma'm, you could put some gates in it. Three or four, maybe. If you'd do that I believe the cowmen'd come around after a while. They'll never *like* your fence, if you'd just show where you weren't – well – *all* dog in the manger – that you wanted to be fenced in but were willing to put up gates for them to get their breachy critters out through – I think they'd accept the fence after a while.'

She moved to the edge of the chair. He knew she was going to get up, say thank-you and good-bye and couldn't think of a solitary word that would pave the way to ask her about going to the barbecue and dance with him on the Fourth.

She stood up. He arose reluctantly, digging for words that eluded him. He glanced down at her. She was looking at him in a strangely intent way. He wondered what kind of an expression was on his face, flushed red he smiled as disarmingly as he knew how.

'I'm glad you stopped by.' It was the simple truth.

'I am, too,' she said, just as simply, then, wonder of wonders, she also blushed. With a wavering smile she left him. He heard the door close without heeding it. His heart was thumping steadily, deeply, with measured pauses between each thump. The office seemed dank and heat-limp suddenly. He scooped up his hat and crossed the little room in three strides, spurs ringing frantically, flung open the door and went out onto the plankwalk.

She was far down the walk, hurrying toward a battered wagon he recognized. Two cowboys were loading sacks of flour and boxes of tinned goods into it from in front of Nolan's Emporium. String-bean-thin Fred Nolan was standing to one side with a pencil, marking things off on a slip of paper as they were loaded. He raised a perspiring face when she came up. With an inward pang Brandon saw the merchant's face break out all over with a beaming smile.

'Well?'

Brandon started, swung his head with a snapping movement. Guilt drenched him inwardly. Charley sat there on his big bay horse, as impassively thoughtful as ever.

'Did you ask her?'

'You cussed spy,' Brandon said, and stepped down into the roadway's dust, went trudging across the way toward the Drover's.

Inside it was cool, mellow-shady, strong smelling. Frosty cast him a sidelong glance and reached for an ale glass. 'Hot out,' he said. It was his all-time conversation opener. The only time it changed was when winter came. Then he would say: 'Cold out.'

Brandon took the ale and dropped a coin. 'Yeah.'

'How's the baby?'

'It wasn't mine,' Brandon said sharply.

'Just askin',' Frosty said, stony-faced. 'Was that its mother?'

'No,' Brandon said. He set the glass down and frowned at it. 'Well – not exactly.'

'Oh. Aunt, huh?'

Brandon shuffled his feet. 'No, not exactly. She got the kid from some folks she knew back East that died.'

'The hell. Funny kind of present, wasn't it?'

Brandon drained off the last of his glass and regarded Frosty coolly. 'You're a nosey cuss,' he said.

'Saved your bacon with that milk though, didn't I?' Frosty sounded reproachful. 'She was as pretty as a yearlin' filly, wasn't she?'

'It was a him, not a her.'

'Not the baby, Brandy, the girl. What's her name? Never seen her around Fort Parker before.'

'Grant.'

Frosty's mouth was open. It stayed open. His eyes batted several times. 'Not old Beasely Grant's heir?'

'Yeah. She and her brother. He's a rawhider, but he's still young. Maybe he'll learn before somebody pins his ears back.'

Frosty didn't appear to be listening. He filled another glass with ale, set it before Brandon, looked down at the draught spigot, gave a little shrug and drew off a glass for himself. After he'd downed a few sups he said: 'Spanners were in here an hour or so ago.'

Brandon looked up. Frosty's eyes were level with his own. They looked calculatingly sly. 'Oh?'

'They'd been to see you, Brandy. They weren't in a very good state of mind.'

'Go on.'

'They were going to Bow and talk to Jared Hoxey about the fence those Grants have put up. Pretty sore about it.'

'Loaded for bear, were they?'

'Not for bear,' Frosty said. 'For war.'

Charley Belton came ambling up and the conversation died there. Brandon knew all he had to know anyway. Frosty set up a glass for Charley and went down the bar where an old gaffer was thumping the counter with a goldheaded cane.

Charley gargled his ale to cut the heat-scorch, set the glass aside and peered at Brandon's face. 'You don't look happy, Brandy,' he said.

'I'm not. The Spanners were in town over that fence of hers.'

'I figured they would be one of these days. Saw Hoxey working cattle near Indian Caves on my way in. We had a cup of chuckwagon coffee. He was madder'n a wet hen about it.'

'That's where the Spanner boys went. Out to see Hoxey.'

Charley finished his ale and leaned both elbows on the counter. 'You've got the makings of a first-class scrap shaping up, Brandy,' he said.

'I believe it. What did Jared say?'

'Asked me if I'd seen the fence. I said I had. He asked about Old Man Grant's successors. I told him about the girl – sort of made the boy out just a horse's rear-end. Too young to shoot, to old to slap. He – well – you know Jared Hoxey. Tough old devil; owned Bow for thirty years or so and a free-range man from the toes up.'

'Yeah,' Brandon said dryly. 'One of the

old-timers. Believes a gun's the best way to settle anything and everything.' He turned, leaned his elbows and back on the counter and gazed disconsolately around the nearly empty saloon. 'Oh hell,' he said.

'Trouble, boy, you got it.'

'Looks that way.'

'Did you ask her?' Charley said with sudden casualness.

'What?'

Charley made a rasping grunt. 'Brandy, if you don't, I'm going to.'

Brandon lifted his hat, mopped a sleeve over his pale forehead and replaced the hat. 'Oh – her.' He sucked in his underlip and scowled. 'Go ahead.'

Charley regarded Brandon's profile without speaking for a time then he too turned and leaned on the bartop. 'You saw her first,' he said.

'She came in to-day. She was over at Nolan's just before I came in here.'

'I know. I saw her.'

'She might still be over there.'

'She is.'

'Then,' Brandon said quietly, a trifle lightly, 'go ask her.'

Without another word Charley Belton walked away from the bar. Brandon watched him go through the louvered doors. That feeling was behind his belt again, only bigger than before. With it was a gorge of something very close to dislike for Charley Belton. Feeling miserable he crossed the saloon, went out onto the plankwalk under the overhang and lost the battle not to look.

She was up on the seat. Charley was standing in the road talking to her, his head thrown back. Her profile was to Brandon. With no effort he imagined the deep blue of her eyes on Charley's face. The curling lilt of her mouth as she talked. The little scattering of sun-dust – the freckles. He turned away.

There weren't many people out. Folks usually tried to get all their chores finished before the sun got overhead. The country writhed with heat. The nights were beautiful, full of dry-grass perfume and soothing warmth, but the days were a curse.

He walked past the stores and crossed the road to his office, went around in back and took off his shirt, grasped the old manure fork and began to dung out the lean-to again. His two horses, the grulla and the black, watched him idly, switching their tails at the hordes of flies.

He worked hard until sunset, locked up the office and went across to the barbershop, gave two bits for the key to the tub room and had a long, cool bath, re-dressed and, more miserable than ever, went to his room over the Drover's.

Two days passed like that. Days that blended into one another so that he wasn't aware of their passing until the evening of the second day Jared Hoxey, owner of the Bow outfit, came stumping into the office just as Brandon was getting ready to lock up.

'Evenin', Brandy.'

'Evenin', Jared. Have a chair.'

Hoxey was bull-necked, red-faced, with a look of quiet authority and ageless strength to him. He was grizzled with years but not bowed by them. He shucked his doeskin roping gloves and dropped heavily into the slat-bottomed chair.

'Been talkin' to the Spanner boys about that fence, Brandy.'

'And?' Brandon said.

Hoxey looked close at him. 'You look a little peaked, Brandy.'

Brandon felt blood surging into his head. In a quiet, stony way he said, 'I'll live. What's on your mind?'

Hoxey rolled the gloves in his fist. 'That goddamned fence. It's got to come down.'

'Who says so?'

Hoxey looked at Brandon with the sharp, close look again. He hesitated over his answer. 'Well – it cuts the range in two. They got no right to do that.'

Brandon leaned on the desk. His pleasant, open face was set in line that didn't become it. 'Jared, they own the land just like you own yours. If you built a fence the law couldn't stop you as long as it was on your own land. Those Grants have the same right and you know it.'

'But, man,' Jared Hoxey protested. 'We never *had* such a damned thing before. Why, Beasely'd pop out of his grave if he knew what they was doing.'

'Doesn't change a thing,' Brandon said implacably. 'Old Man Grant's gone. They own the place and they can fence it if they want to.'

Hoxey lapsed into silence. His face got slowly redder. His squinted eyes burnt brightly behind their little puckers of flesh. 'Brandy: I told Fat I'd talk to you first. See if maybe the two of us couldn't make some sense out of this. Now I don't think you want to go along with us.'

'It's not a matter of going along,' Brandon said. 'It's right and wrong as I see it – that's what I'm paid to watch out for. That's what I'm going to do.'

Hoxey waited even longer before he spoke again. 'They ain't even putting gates in it.'

'You seen it, Jared?'

The little eyes flashed. 'No, course not. Don't have to. Fat and Ed and Jim rode the full length of it. They said there wasn't a gate in it anywhere.' Hoxey, studying the younger features across the desk from him, altered his tone a little. 'Now, Brandy – you know that ain't right. Least they could do would be to put gates in there so's the boys could get their critters out. Now then, don't that sound reasonable to you?'

'Why don't you go out there and tell them that?'

'You know 'em best,' Hoxey shot right back. 'Besides; as the law they'd listen to you where they'd pay no attention to me or the Spanners.'

Brandon shook his head and stood up. 'I'd be using my badge to make a point for the cattlemen by doing that. You know that, Jared.'

'Well, dammit all,' Hoxey said arising, flexing one leg gingerly. 'Who's paying you anyway, if it ain't the cowmen?'

'But not just to serve them. Cowmen are the biggest taxpayers but they aren't the only people in the country. Jared, if you want gates in that fence go out there and reason with her with – *them* – I'm not going out there at all.' He said the last seven words with enough vehemence to startle the older man.

Hoxey peered up at him. He looked perplexed. 'All right, Brandy. Now let me tell you something. Them folks can't come into this country and think they're going to change everything. It just won't go down. I'll go see the sheriff over at the County Seat if I got to, but one way or another that fence's got to go – now you mark my words.'

Brandon picked up his hat, dumped it on the back of his head and stared at the Bow-ranch owner. 'Are you making a threat, Jared?' he asked.

'And if I am?'

Brandon's voice cracked like a bullwhip. 'If you are I'll throw you in the cess so damned quick you'll never know what hit you.'

Hoxey's Adam's-apple jumped. He pulled on his gloves but never took his eyes off Brandon's face. When he was across the room, one hand on the drawbar of the door, he said: 'Brandy, for some reason you got a burr under your saddleblanket.' Then he left.

The next day was the Fourth. It was dusty-hot and people from all over the Fort Parker country came to town. There were wagons and buggies and horsemen everywhere. There was noise and confusion, dust and barking dogs, even a few random shots which brought Brandon out of his office. Of course he didn't find the exuberant shooters; he didn't try to very hard.

All the saloons were full of yelping, stomping, perspiring men. The women-folk were out at the picnic-grounds where some wind-bent old cottonwoods stood, unpacking hampers of food, yelling at their children and slapping at the flies and ants. Fort Parker was a beehive on the Fourth.

A huge trench gave off tantalizing odors of barbecued beef. Sweating men with red faces and fluffy garters holding up their candy-striped silk shirt sleeves used pitchforks to turn the slabs of meat. Frosty Turner was out at the grounds with a flimsy tarp over a hastily made plank-bar. He had six oaken kegs on hand and a personal thirst almost equal to all six from serving the flow of customers he had.

In the morning there was, of course, a big parade. Everyone was in it, just about. Ranch buggies loaded with kids and men, and some of the women, wound like a funeral procession through the dust, stirring it into spirals that flattened at knee-height and mushroomed out, heavy, dun-brown, cow-country dust almost thick enough to chew.

Brandon stood under the overhang of his office and watched the vehicles and careening horsemen go by. He knew every brand burned or painted upon a wagon or a buggy. He also knew most of the young-old faces of the riders with their elegantly curled, waxed and perfumed mustaches.

He saw the entire procession, tasted the dust, waved at the kids, without smiling once. Afterwards he drifted with the tide of people to the picnic ground. There, Frosty, harassed, cherry-pink and soggy looking, caught his eye and set aside a foaming glass for him. He drank it – it was tepid – paid Frosty and strolled among the picnickers.

It seemed to Brandon that the kids and dogs fared the best. The adults worked as hard at relaxing, having a big Fourth, as they would have worked at home bringing in cattle or haying. He wasn't hungry but he had to stop four times and eat a little with people who hailed him.

He went out beyond the big old trees, stood in their shade and watched the competing riders at their impromptu rodeo. A Bow rider he knew flashed by on a good little chestnut stud-horse and tossed Brandon the start of a quick, friendly salute, that died in mid-wave. A quick, embarrassed look fled over the rider's features then he was lost in the dust. Brandon looked after him, hand held up. Odd. No – not exactly. Not after the way he'd talked to Jared. He moved back deeper into the shade, plucked a wizened stalk of dead grass and chewed it watching.

The afternoon dragged for Brandon, but from the sounds and smells he was the only one it dragged for. Later, about four o'clock, it seemed that every mother and squaw on earth had dumped her kids upon the town with all restrictions removed. There were kids of all ages and sizes everywhere.

Brandon threaded his way through them as far as the dance pavilion – built seven years before by the G. A. R. – and there he listened to the musicians tuning up or warming up, whatever they did to coax decency out of the most improbable assortment of instruments the town had ever seen. Two perspiring men

– one was Fred Nolan, of Nolan's Emporium ('Best In The West') profanely trying to get wilted red-white-and-blue bunting to hang artistically upon the front of the musicians' platform. Brandon helped them for a while, then a wispy old man came up and tugged at his sleeve.

'Fight yonder, Marshal,' the oldster said excitedly. 'Dog-fight, 'twixt two bucks.'

Brandon went up the dusty roadway, through the traffic where a large hooting congregation of men were circling around something that was causing an awful lot more dust.

'Give way, fellers,' he said, elbowing his way. 'Come on – dammit – let's have a little slack in there.'

When he was in the forefront of the spectator-ring he saw them on the ground, shirts torn, pale flesh contrasting weirdly with their bronzed faces, gasping and pummelling, eye-gouging and ear-chawing. He knew them both. One was Arty Fortin, son of old Henry Fortin who ranched southwest of town, and the other one was a brawny Wagonwheel rider named Sims. Both young and full of vinegar.

He bent and caught young Fortin by the britches, braced and gave a mighty heave that sucked Fortin right out from under the heavier cowboy. Hauled him up and shoved him roughly toward the laughing bystanders.

'Hold him,' he said. They did, a dozen strong arms closing about Fortin's panting body.

Brandon watched the surprised Wagonwheeler get to his knees, looking around. 'Get up, mister,' he said. 'Go get another shirt and no more fighting or you'll get drug in.'

The cowboy came up slowly, throwing his head. He turned. His face was as red as a beet, the eyes bloodshot and vicious looking. 'Keep your damned nose out o' this, tin-badge.'

Brandon had both thumbs hooked into his shell-belt. He removed them, let them hang at his sides. He had looked into a lot of faces like that one. Without raising his voice he said: 'Go duck your head in the water-trough, pardner – while you've got a head to duck.'

The Wagonwheeler moved toward Brandon. Very suddenly two men pushed out of the crowd. One was half as big as the battered cowboy. He grabbed the fighter's arm and half whirled him off balance. In a nasal voice that cut through the dust he said: 'Go duck your head!'

That ended it.

The crowd dispersed, laughing. The short, wiry man walked over to Brandon. He wore no smile. 'He'll be all right, Brandy. He's a good feller.' Small, steely eyes looked up.

'Sure,' Brandy said, looking down at the

Wagonwheel foreman. 'Good thing for one of us you stepped out, Sam.'

The foreman cocked his head to one side. 'This time it was, Brandy.'

Brandon felt puzzled. 'What do you mean by that, Sam?' he said.

'This time there was going to be a fight. It's a good thing you had someone to step in. Next time you mayn't be so lucky.'

'What next time are you talking about?'

'That fence, Brandy,' the shorter man said, then he turned away, went down toward the dance pavilion with other riders who were hanging back waiting for him.

Brandon walked over to the sidewalk.

The sun set reluctantly. Its parting salvoes of light were slivers of endless brilliance, slanting down from the distant mountains. They bathed Fort Parker and the country-side in a mellow twilight. People came to life. Men went by on the plankwalk yawning, faces puffy and clothing rumpled. They'd had a nap after the picnic. Brandon watched them flow southward, toward the pavilion. A little later, when the last long fingerlings of light were gone, music started. First there was the National Anthem, played with considerable vehemence. Next came a deafening square-dance. The music was loud enough, but the shrieks and howls, the hoots and guffaws, made the air vibrate with sound. Brandon trailed the last of the crowd down there; walked with the grandmothers and toddlers, the old gaffers and the raffish dogs.

And he saw them.

Marti out there on the platform in a gingham dress, her hair swept back with the little green ribbon around it, her face radiant, blue eyes flashing with a cold fire, her mouth parted and her little nose tilted up toward Charley, who loomed over her with a warm and self-conscious look to him. Neither of them saw Brandon, he thought, standing down among the old people, the kids and the dogs.

She whirled through the square-dance like a miniature cloud with curves. Twice Brandon saw her ankles when she spun. It made his neck red. The music stopped. People drifted noisily toward the planked-off outer bank of the pavilion. A man stood up in a limp white coat that was someone else's – the sleeves nearly covered his fingers – and orated. Brandon didn't hear him. He was watching *them*. Marti listened to Charley, but her eyes were never still. Brandon watched their path as they swept the crowd and once, when they swung close he felt himself drawing inward, away from their gaze.

Profiled sideways, full figure, she was far and away the prettiest girl on the pavilion. He stoically compared her to the others. To Jemima Fortin, supposedly the prettiest girl in the Fort Parker country. Jemima couldn't hold a candle. The eyes were on him. Full force and unmoving, he couldn't look away. It lasted a whole lifetime telescoped into five seconds, then her mouth was lifting, curling upwards in that way she had. It moved softly. He had no idea what the words were. She nodded toward him. Charley was cutting around her, blocking off Brandon's view. He came over to the edge of the pavilion without smiling at all. There was something in his tone Brandon didn't try to fathom.

'Next one's a round-dance, Brandy.'

That was all he said. Then he vaulted over the pavilion railing and disappeared rearward through the crowd.

She was still looking at him with that guileless, small smile. He jumped over the railing with a fever in his face and walked toward her. When he was close he could see the way the sturdy little pulse in her throat was pumping. Hard and fast.

'Ma'm?' he said, with a funny little bow, all angles and awkwardness.

'I'd love to,' she said.

They stood side by side waiting for the music to begin again. He felt like a panther waiting to spring. She looked as cool, as relaxed and thoroughly happy as a girl could look.

'Marshal? Weren't you at the picnic?'

'Yes. I didn't see you and Charley there.'

'We arrived late,' she said innocently.

The funny feeling behind his belt was insufferably painful. 'Lots of dust,' he said vaguely.

'Charley said there would be. That's why I left the baby home. Milton didn't want to come, anyway. He was mad.'

'About Charley coming by for you?'

She nodded her head, turned and looked up at him. 'It's so much fun, isn't it? Don't you love Fourth of July celebrations?'

'Yes,' he said solemnly, without conviction.

'We have them back in Indiana, too, but they're mostly marching parades. This is so – so – unrestrained. So wholesome and sort of – free.'

He gazed at her, and then, with great finality and ease, he knew what he always felt when he was around her. Protective. She wasn't any bigger than minute, but sturdy. Strong as a miniature stud-horse. Rounded, with abundance, but without a *super*-abundance. Protective... The music started.

His hands were damp. He rubbed them surreptitiously down his pantlegs, then held them out. She slid into his arms like she'd been molded for them. The funny feeling was stronger. She was like holding a flake of meadow hay, that light. He danced – and he'd never been a good dancer before – like they were floating. He didn't even hear the music, which was noteworthy in itself, for the musicians were blowing and beating and strumming as though their welfare in the Hereafter depended, not upon quality, but upon quantity.

Neither of them said a word for a full minute, then she looked up at him. 'You're a good dancer, Sher – Marshal.'

'I've got a name,' he said scratchily, with a lump in his throat.

'I know; it's Brandy. I like it. Not brandy, the name. I've got a name, too.'

He couldn't say it. The lump was too big.

They danced half-way across the pavilion. Her hair was under his nose. It tickled and itched, but he wouldn't do anything about it; wouldn't even turn his head.

'Brandy, didn't you *want* to dance?'

He looked down at her swiftly. Their eyes weren't more than seven inches apart. 'Yes, I wanted to.'

'Why didn't you come inside the pavilion, then? I saw you ages before I sent Charley over.'

'Did you?' A tremor rippled the length of him.

'Well – I didn't know.'

She searched his face. 'Is there someone – I mean – maybe you would rather not be seen dancing with me. Another girl, possibly?'

He thought of his moonlight drives with Jemima Fortin in the liverybarn buggy, but they weren't anything. He hadn't even touched her; held her hand even. 'No,' he said frankly. 'There isn't another girl here. I don't have one, as a matter of fact.'

'Well, the fence then. Maybe you didn't want people to–'

In a stronger tone he said: 'Let's not talk about that cussed fence just this once. All right?'

She didn't answer. She snuggled up close to him, put her head against his chest. They continued to move like a cloud, far removed from everyone, everything. Then the music stopped and they were adrift, the spell broken. She flushed and looked up at him open-eyed; he, awkward, breathless, conscious of the night's warmth. She took his hand and led him along. When they got back to the railing Charley was there with a mug of tepid ale in his hand.

Brandon nodded and noticed Charley's usual bland expression was as usual, and felt nothing toward Charley like he had felt before.

Marti dropped Brandon's hand and smiled at Charley. 'Your dance next, Charley, if you want it.'

They talked desultorily through a pall of separate thoughts and sometimes the conversation got all crossed up, but when the music started and Charley, still with his inscrutable expression, whirled her away,

Brandon caught her eye around Charley's arm. She just stared at him.

The pavilion was full of people. He saw very few faces that he didn't recognize; hadn't known since childhood. Not many newcomers had emigrated to the Fort Parker country in the past few years. It was an isolated land in many ways, like most cattle country was.

He watched Sam Morton, foreman of Bow, dancing with Jemima Fortin. She was at least four inches taller than Sam. Once, their eyes met over the top of Sam's head. Brandon smiled, tentatively. Jemima, her flashing black eyes wide, was gazing speculatively, woodenly, at him. Frosty Turner came over, mopping his extra high forehead with a huge square of blue bandana-cloth.

'Man! I'm glad this only happens once a year.'

'You make money,' Brandon said, ducking his head to get a glimpse of Marti.

'Aw – money's fine. I got nothing against it. A man can be a damned sight happier with it than 'thout it, but I like to prance a little, too.'

'Hire a helper.'

'I just did, temporary. Now I'm here to cut a buck. Say – isn't that Jemima Fortin dancin' with Sam out there.'

'Yes.' He saw Marti. She was looking straight at him from half-way across the pavilion. Her face, flushed, looked composed. Set in marble, expressionless. He returned her stare without thinking that others might notice it and, strangely, she didn't seem to care, either.

'Think I'll snag Jemima,' Frosty said musingly, tucking away the monstrous handkerchief. Brandon didn't answer as Frosty started across the pavilion. The music stopped. Frosty stood stock-still for a moment then gave his head a wag and returned to Brandon's side.

'Hell of a note.'

She came across the pavilion holding Charley's fingers like she'd held his and Brandon got the impression she was deliberately avoiding his stare now. When Charley swung her gently toward the railing Frosty craned his neck in a way that annoyed Brandon, and smiled so wide his face threatened to crack.

'Howdy, ma'm. Haven't seen you since that day – in the – saloon.' Two sets of eyes were boring into him. He drew back a little, looking confused, then craned his neck again and Brandon saw it coming. For once he beat another man to the punch by being bold.

'Can I have the next dance, Marti?'

It just slipped out. He heard himself say it and was rooted to the pavilion floor... 'Marti?'

She nodded.

Brandon relaxed, feeling triumphant. He

even shot a sidelong glance at the disappointed face of Frosty Turner. Charley Belton looked very casually over their heads toward the crowd.

'Want me to fetch you an ale, Brandy?'

'No thanks, Charley.'

'Reckon I'll get one, then. You want a lemonade, Marti?' She smiled and shook her head. Belton's gaze traveled to Frosty's perspiring face. 'Why'n't you come along, Frosty?' They went. Charley, with his fingers like a big bronze vice around Frosty's arm, propelling him. Brandon turned sideways towards Marti.

'It's hot, isn't it?' he said, inanely.

She smiled. It made him feel like some kind of a conspirator. 'You finally got it out, didn't you?'

'The name? Yes. It just sort of slid out.' He straightened up when a Wagonwheeler swung in close with a red-faced grin.

'Next dance, ma'm?'

'I'm sorry, it's promised.'

'Sure,' the rider said with a deep look of genuine appreciation at her. 'I'll be back. Thanks.'

'The hell you will,' Brandon said under his breath without returning the man's civil nod.

'What did you say?'

He floundered. 'Oh, the name. Yes'm.'

She regarded him with a pixeyish look,

then laughed. He hadn't heard her laugh before and gazed at her wonderingly.

'Now?'

The music had started. He moved jerkily like he had before, until she was snuggled up close, then they floated. The same perfume from her hair, the same funny feeling, the same…

'Brandy?'

'Yes'm?'

'I think Charley's wonderful, don't you?'

He said 'Yes' very flatly and she moved her head back to look up at him. It was almost dark. Someone was going around the bandstand hanging lanterns on nails. Very suddenly she stopped dancing and pushed back from him a little. 'Come on, let's walk.'

Thinking his glum expression had angered her, he followed along like a led-dog. They left the pavilion, threaded their way past people who looked, then swung to look again, and got as far as the deserted plankwalk. Scattered up and down both sides of the road in the flagrant, gloomy warmth, were other strollers. Most of them hand in hand. She felt for his fingers, grasped them, and he marveled that her touch was so cool and strangely warm at the same time. They walked northward almost to the end of town, where the plankwalk ended, and there she stopped, gazing up into the night. The stars winked on and off. They were so clear-cut he could almost hear them crackle.

'Isn't it beautiful?'

He wasn't looking up when he answered. 'The prettiest thing I've ever seen.'

She turned toward him and it happened; just happened. He was kissing her and she was standing on her tiptoes with her arms around his neck. It was a warm, tingling kind of a kiss, too delightful to ever end, but it ended when she rocked down and stepped back, looking up at him.

She had her hand halfway to her lips when she said, 'For heaven's sake – alive!'

He looked perfectly and astoundedly blank. Very weakly he echoed her with, 'Yes. Funny thing to have – happen.'

'It certainly happened though, didn't it?'

'Golly,' he said, still in the weak, distant voice.

'We'd better go back, Brandy.'

'Now? Right now?'

Her eyes, darker from the night and from something else as well, were like liquid freshets still in mid-stream. 'I think – we should. Shouldn't we?'

'Marti? You talked about Charley.'

'I said he was nice.'

'You said he was wonderful.'

'Well; isn't he, Brandy?'

'Then I'm sorry I did that. Kissed you.'

Her hand fell away. She seemed to stand more erect. 'Brandy – Brandy. I meant he was wonderful because he took that man away. That balding man with the blue handkerchief, they went away – don't you see?'

'Well,' he said. 'They went to get some ale.'

She didn't answer him right away. 'Brandy, Charley took that man away so we wouldn't be – so we'd be together. Oh, come on. Let's walk.'

He trudged northward out beyond town with her for a ways before he stopped a second time. 'Wait a second. You mean Charley *knew?*'

'Yes. I told him I wanted to talk to you.'

'Oh.' His mouth held the shape of the sound after he uttered it. 'Oh. I see.'

'Do you? Are you still sorry you kissed me?'

'To be real honest, Marti, I never really was.'

'Then do it again.'

He did. Bent down to meet her and she tiptoed to meet him, and he kissed her with a drumroll of heartbeats hammering in his ears.

She worked free and stood motionless without looking at him. Her voice didn't sound right. 'I think we'd better go back now.'

Neither of them spoke until they were almost to the pavilion, then Charley Belton came through the crowd toward them. His face had a strange, anxious expression on it as he gazed from one to the other. Almost brusquely he took Marti's arm. 'Feller over in your office wants to see you, Brandy. I'll take care of Marti.'

He was left standing there. Once she turned to look back at him with a midnight-blue stare, very grave, very solemn, then she was lost in the crowd. Brandon's protective feeling had become a part of him. It would never die.

He went across the roadway, angled around the horse-racks and entered his office. The lamp had been turned up. He looked at the solitary man in the room and recognized him. It was one of the clean-shaven cowboys from the Grant place. Something ominous brushed lightly against Brandon's awareness.

'You wanted to see me?'

'Yeah. The other big feller said to tell you first, not her.'

'What other big feller? You mean Charley Belton?'

'I reckon. Don't know his name. Big feller you rode out to the ranch with one time.'

'All right, that's Charley Belton. What did he say for you to tell me?'

'Somebody shot Milt.'

Brandon sat down solidly. He put his hat carefully on the desk in front of him without looking at the rider. 'Tell me about it.'

'Ain't much to tell. We was playin' poker over at the house. On the veranda so's we

71

could hear the baby if it commenced crying. He got tired of playin', asked me to stick around the house after the game broke up and watch the kid, then he saddled up and rode off. 'Bout an hour later I was having a smoke, the other fellers had gone back over to the bunkhouse, and I thought I heard the echo of a gunshot. I got the boys an' we went over toward the fence. Sure enough, we seen his horse standing there and lying face down in the grass was Milt.'

'Dead?'

'Nope, but not far from it. We got him back to the ranch in a wagon. He's there now. I rode in to find Miz Grant an' tell her.'

'You've got to get the doctor,' Brandon said mechanically.

'I already have. Sawbones left town while I was hunting Miz Grant around the pavilion. She wasn't there and this big feller nailed me when I asked him about her. I told him what happened and he said for me to come over here and wait for you – that he'd look you and her up for me.'

'Where was he hit?'

'I didn't stay to look,' the rider said, 'but he's got blood all to hell over everything. The wagon, his shirts and pants – he's hard hit all right, I can tell you that.'

Brandon rummaged in a desk drawer for his tobacco sack. His hands were shaking.

Chapter Three

It was darker than the inside of a well when Brandon got to the Grant place, but the old house was leaking lights from every crack. He recognized the doctor's rig out front, the old mare sleeping in the shafts. Three men on the veranda were sooty silhouettes. Two had cherry-red cigarette-ends glowing. He swung down, tied the grulla and went up the steps.

'Howdy,' a voice said from the porch gloom.

'Howdy. How is he?'

'Don't know. Doc's with him.'

Brandon looked at the faces, recognized one as the older man who had been in the wagon when he and Charley had gone out to examine the fence. The face was foxlike, secretive looking, as though its owner was a person full of small anxieties, spring-like tensions.

He went into the house, chucked his hat on the kitchen table and prowled around until he found them in a back bedroom. There was blood on the floor and in a sweeping curve, low, on the north wall. The doctor ignored him and Milt looked like a piece of melted wax, covered with blankets

73

in the bed. His eyes were closed, lips bluish, cheeks sunken, dead looking.

Brandon moved around to the foot of the bed, stared down. The doctor's hands moved without wasted motion. Each movement meant something, did something. Brandon turned away finally, thinking Milt was a goner.

The pile of clothing lay in a messy heap. He knelt and carefully laid them out on the floor as though a man were in them, face down. The bullet apparently had caught Milt across the back. Perhaps he was moving when it struck him. The shirt-back was torn in a straight, shredded line, right across the shoulders. Brandon hunkered, thinking, reconstructing. It hadn't been meant for a warning shot, not that close and that high. Whoever had tugged it off had meant to kill the boy. Shoot him through the lights from behind. He rocked back on his heels, sought Milt's gun, found it, flicked open the ejection slide, spun the cylinder, then smelled the barrel. It hadn't been fired in a long time. He got up and went back to the foot of the bed. The doctor was finishing up. He raised a tired face.

'Bad one.'

'Yeah. What does it look like to you, Doc?'

The doctor went back to sluicing blood off his hands and wrists in the washbasin. 'Well, I'd say the man was fairly close. That the boy was moving when it hit him, maybe hunched over or something just as the bushwhacker fired.'

'Any chance of it being an accident?' Brandon asked, regarding the waxen face, the motionless eyelids.

'No. Not the way I see it, Brandy.' The doctor wiped thoughtfully. He didn't look up. 'There's been a lot of talk about the fence these people have put up. You've undoubtedly heard more of it than I have. The riders told me he went out by the fence. My guess would be that he came upon someone in the act of cutting it. They shot him.'

'When will he be able to talk?'

The doctor gazed at the still form. 'There's a very good chance – never. He's lost a lot of blood. The shock was bad. Now – if he gets an infection...'

'Won't he be conscious again?'

'I have no idea. I've seen cases like this where they never come back. Fever sets in and they stay out of their heads until they die.'

Brandon gazed at the dead-looking face. 'What I'm trying to figure out is whether there's any point in me hanging around here the rest of the night. If he'll come around long enough to tell me whether he saw anyone or not.'

'I'm sorry, Brandy, I can't answer that.' The doctor's gaze swung to his face. 'But guessing – just guessing – I don't see how he could snap out of it until tomorrow morning, if then.'

'Thanks.' Brandon started to turn away. 'Doc, you'll stick close, won't you? Watch out for that infection?'

'Yes, but he isn't my only patient, you know.'

'I know. You'll do your best though.'

'Certainly.'

'Thanks.'

He walked back through the house to the veranda. The night air was cooling. Irrelevantly he thought it was very late, past midnight, probably.

'How is he?'

Brandon turned. It was the granite-looking older man with the flaring nostrils and faded, secretive-looking eyes. He was holding a tobacco sack out. Brandon shook his head at the sack. 'No thanks. He's not too good, the doctor says.'

'Yeah. We thought he was dead till we got him inside under a lantern.'

Brandon fixed the man with a stare. 'Were you one of those that brought him back?'

'Yeah.'

'How about getting a horse and showing me exactly where you found him.'

'Now? It's darker'n hell.'

Brandon wondered which of two ideas prompted that answer. Fear that the rawhider might still be out there, or just the fact that it was too dark to see. He leaned against a porch upright.

'Yeah, now.'

'All right,' the rider said, throwing his companions a quick look. 'Be right back.'

While he waited, Brandon asked the others what they knew and got the answers he expected. He'd already heard it all from the young rider back in town. One cowboy crumpled a cigarette in his fingers and said: 'Miz Grant know yet?'

Brandon nodded. 'By now she does.' He saw the wispy man riding toward them and went down the steps to his horse, flicked the reins up and stepped aboard, swung around and rode stirrup with the cowboy.

The coolness seemed to lie in layers. When they skirted close to a landswell the west side was always warm. When they went over a slope and down the east side it was cooler. A coyote sounded a long way off. Something waddling-fat made a rustling sound as it grunted and snuffled trying to get out of their path. The cowboy's gun slid out like lightning.

Brandon growled at the man. 'Porcupine. Don't shoot it. We can't stop to bury it now and if there's anyone around they'll hear the shot.'

The cowboy held his gun. Tracked the animal with it, but he didn't shoot. 'I hate them damned things,' he said. 'Worst job on earth's when you got to rope cattle and pull them quills out'n their noses.'

Dourly Brandon said: 'Worse to kill them and leave them laying than it is to let them go. Quills from dead ones'll lie in the grass for years. If you can't bury or burn them, better to let them go. Critters get more quills from dead ones than live ones.'

The cowboy holstered his gun. For a long time neither man said anything, then the rider swerved a little, heading southeast. Brandon followed his example.

'Marshal; you reckon that might have been accidental, some way?'

'I don't know. It might have been, but I don't see how. Hard enough to hit a man on a horse in broad daylight.'

'Yeah. Well, listen; we were talking it over back at the ranch. I used to work for Old Man Grant, but them others haven't been around the ranch long. Now then – if that tomfool fence is going to start a range-war, they want to draw their pay and ride on.' The seamed old face turned toward Brandon. It was gray-white in the darkness. 'You can't blame them,' the old cowboy added.

'No, I don't blame them, but I've got nothing to do with that, either. How much farther?'

The rider studied Brandon's face a second before he turned away, raised an arm and said, 'Over yonder 'bout a half a mile. I can see the fence from here.'

Brandon looked. With no rust on it yet, the new wire shone with a dull, watery paleness. He kept staring at it until the rider reined up, squinted downward, dismounted and walked ahead leading his horse. Brandon got down, too.

'Here it is. There – see that mashed down grass? Over there's the blood. Darker spot there.'

Brandon, thumbs hooked into his shell-belt, studied the ground. He spoke without looking around. 'All right; thanks. You can go back now.'

The cowboy seemed to hesitate, then he mounted, whirled his horse and rode away without another word.

Brandon knelt. Because the light was so poor it took him a long time to figure it out. The horse had shied. He found the tracks before the shot had gone off and afterward. When the bushwhacker's gun had gone off Milt's animal, startled, had given a big shy-ing leap sideways. He ran his fingers over the imprints of the toe-marks. The ground was dark and warm to the touch.

If the bullet hadn't knocked the kid off, the horse probably would have shied out from under him anyway. He moved a little, keeping scrupulously clear of the imprints he was reading.

Milton had landed a good six feet from the horse. Falling, his horse shying, he had probably been thrown that far to the left of the animal. Where he'd landed the grass was matted, so he'd landed hard. And, he hadn't moved. Hadn't even rolled. He was probably unconscious when he hit, then.

Brandon felt the blood. It was like jelly, only darker. Must have happened not more than three hours earlier. He stood up and gazed out beyond the fence, which was about sixty feet away. Unless Brandon's reckonings were crossed up somewhere, the bushwhacker had been across the fence not more than sixty to a hundred yards away. If he'd been closer he wouldn't have wounded the kid, he'd have killed him. Leading his horse around the churned earth he dropped the tie-rope over a post, crawled through the wire and kept off to one side of what he thought must have been the bullet's course.

The land began to lighten, getting a mottled grey color. Surprised, he looked at the horizon. There was a pale, watery blue streak across it. Dawn. He stopped dead still. That much time couldn't have passed, but it had.

He walked closer, watching for tracks. There were none anywhere near the fence. The rawhider had seen the kid fall then, and hadn't gone up to make sure. Back quite a way from the fence he found the faintest imprints of a shod horse. If it hadn't been light he wouldn't have seen them, the ground was so packed, so summer-baked, that even with the light, if the animal hadn't been agitated he wouldn't have been able to make out the sliding, slamming tracks farther back. He knelt. There was some bay hair, summer-short, among the grass tops, held there by the dew.

He arose and stood still, studying the tracks. It was difficult to be sure, but he thought they came from the east, or in the general direction of town. That didn't mean much because yesterday a lot of people had been moving around. He looked back down the land. The sun was beginning to edge up over the rim of the world.

That would make it harder. Maybe the bushwhacker had planned it, figured that with lots of activity his tracks wouldn't mean anything. That is, if he planned it at all. Brandon studied the close-cropped range. As dry and hard as it was, unless the ambusher rode cow trails where there would be dust, he wouldn't leave enough to track him by.

The sun came up like an immense disc of molten gold. It poured heat and smashing daylight down over the world in a great gushing torrent. Brandon could feel the heat almost as soon as he saw the shadows dissolve. Light prickled off grass stems, reflected off tiny flecks of mica in the dust, gave off a golden essence from something closer, not more than twenty feet from him. He bent and peered, then walked closer, gazing downward, bent and picked up the shiny thing. A spent cartridge. A brass casing, .30.30 caliber. He held it between two fingers. The firing pin had been blunt, striking a little higher than center. Winchester carbine. Everyone in the country had at least one of them. He turned from the spot where the casing had been and measured the distance. There was one long, sliding boot track. A skidding looking mark that had nothing definable about it except the impression a foot had made as the leg slid behind the gunman, that, and a worn looking heel. So, the rawhider had knelt to fire. It had been a very deliberate shooting.

Brandon dropped the casing into his pocket and studied the boot mark. Closer scrutiny didn't add anything to what he'd first seen except a tiny depression in the dust where a knee had been. Brandon knelt beside it, pushing one foot behind him. The rawhider's toe hadn't been as far back as his own was; he had been shorter then. Brandon gauged the difference. Maybe five inches shorter.

He arose, looked around the empty land, at the sun, back where his horse stood drowsily across the fence. And started back... She'd be home by now. Probably have Charley with her. The first shock would be past. He climbed through the wire, looped the tie-rope, made it fast, snugged up the reins and mounted. An old cow was calling her calf somewhere to the west of him in a deep-drawn repetitive bellow. He rode back where Milt had fallen and sat there like a carving for several minutes, then struck back overland toward the Grant place.

When he topped over a rolling rib of land he saw a rider on a big bay horse coming toward him. Charley. He rode down into the cool shade and waited. When Charley got close Brandon spoke.

'Got the makings with you, Charley?'

Belton fished out sack and papers and handed them over wordlessly, watched Brandon twist up a cigarette and held out a match, leaning from the saddle.

'Got any ideas, Brandy?'

'A couple. How is she?'

'Danged if I liked my part in that,' Charley said soberly. 'Crying women make me feel like a bully, for some reason.'

'How's the kid; sawbones still there?'

'Yeah, but he was getting ready to leave when I rode over here. The kid's not so good – I don't know about him.'

'Be awful if he dies,' Brandon said with a sinking sensation inside him.

Charley didn't push it. He had a private notion that Milt wouldn't pull through. 'What'd you find?'

83

Brandon dug out the casing and handed it to him. 'This. Some tracks where the raw-hider was when he shot Milt and where Milt fell. His horse shied out from under him.'

Charley studied the casing a long time. 'Won't help much,' he said. 'The pin was hitting a mite higher'n usual, but I reckon half the carbines in the country do that.'

'Yeah. The gunman was maybe half a foot shorter than I am. He was wearing old boots, probably came riding from the east – from the direction of town. He was riding a bay horse.'

'How do you know about the horse?'

'It jumped. I guess when he fired. There was some bay horsehair in the grass.'

'Cow hair, maybe.'

Brandon took a long drag off his cigarette and shook his head. 'Nope; horsehair. Too short and fine, besides it'd have to be a darned light Durham to have hair that color. Durham or milk-cow-cross Grant cattle are all whiteface.'

Charley handed the casing back. 'Want to go to the house?'

'Any sense to it?'

'No,' Charley said. 'She'll want to be alone with him, I expect.'

'Then let's head for town. I'm hungrier'n a bear.'

By the time they were scuffling through the dust of Fort Parker's roadway the sun was hot enough to fry eggs. The town looked dreary and dirty. The signs of revelry were tarnished and droopy looking. A few older boys were working half-heartedly around the pavilion, cleaning up, taking down the bunting. Not many people were abroad. They rode as far as the Marshal's office and around in back to the lean-to. Bandon unsaddled and turned his horse into the corral. Charley led his under the shed, unsaddled and forked some meadow-hay into the cribbed manger. They went around in front and there Brandon stopped, gazing at the listless little town.

'I'll buy you a breakfast, Charley.'

'All right. I'll eat it.'

They went to the Drover's annex and sat at a table. When the food came Charley put his hat on a chair and stretched long legs under the table, looking over at Brandon.

'She sure took it hard.' He shook his head. 'Next time I'll ease out of that chore, believe me. You're her man – that stuff's your responsibility.'

Brandon looked over his fork at Belton. 'You think I am, Charley?' he asked softly.

Charley hunched over his plate hiding his face. 'Cut it out,' he said. 'She told me – when we were dancing. Anyway, I saw it coming long before that.' He swallowed and stabbed at a piece of bacon. 'She's the best thing that could happen to a man. Here,

85

have some toast.' He shoved the dish toward Brandon. 'What are you going to do about the kid?'

'Find the rawhider,' Brandon said simply.

Charley didn't speak again until they were outside standing on the plankwalk in the sun. Then he said, 'Well, I hope you make it, but you're going to sweat a little, I think, before you do.'

'Come on over to the office.'

Lying on the floor where the postmaster had shoved it under the door was a long envelope smudged with dust. Brandon grunted when he picked it up. 'From the sheriff,' he said, tearing open the flap. He read the brief note with lowering brows, sighed and handed it to Charley, perched on the edge of his desk and stared at the wall.

'I'll bet you ten-to-one Jared Hoxey rode over and talked him into that.'

Charley put the letter on the desk and went over to the slat-bottomed chair digging for his tobacco sack. 'Nothing wrong with it that I can see. He just wants you to ride over for a talk with him.'

'Yeah, that's all. He'll want to talk about the fence.'

'That's all anyone talks about any more.'

'But if I ride over there – if I started right now, Charley – I couldn't be back until tomorrow night.'

'Well, what about it? The world won't

come apart before you get back.'

'Won't it? Milt got shot last night. There's going to be hell to pay around here from now on. How do I know Hoxey didn't plan it this way? Maybe he even thought I'd of gotten that letter last night or yesterday, wouldn't be around when the kid got hit.'

Charley lit his cigarette. 'You're saying Jared shot the kid, Brandy.'

Brandon swung his leg limply. 'He could have. I thought about him out there. His height is about right. That roping horse of his is bay.'

'Aw hell,' Charley said irritably. 'My horse is bay, too, and Jared isn't the only short feller in the country.'

'How about the rest of it? Him thinking I might not be around?'

Charley got up and threw his cigarette into the spittoon. 'Bull!' he said shortly. 'You've got it in your head that he did it, that's all. Hell; if you'd been gone, maybe no one would've shot the punk and then again maybe ten men would've. That doesn't prove anything. You better ride over to Fallbrook and talk to the sheriff.'

Brandon had been watching Charley's face. 'On one condition,' he said. 'You be deputy Town Marshal while I'm gone.'

Charley's head came up in astonishment. 'Are you crazy, Brandy?'

'Then I stay right here.'

87

'The sheriff'll be sore as a boiled owl.'

'I can quit, Charley. Quit and hire out to Marti.'

Charley's face got a pinched look to it. His eyes stayed on Brandon's face without blinking for a long moment, then he said: 'You got it bad. It's cross-fired your common sense, Brandy. You ought to take a long ride this evenin' all by yourself. Sort your thoughts out.' He paused, then bobbed his head slightly. 'All right. It's only until tomorrow night, anyway. Give me the badge.'

Brandon saddled the black horse and rode southwest out of town. The heatwaves danced and pulsed in arid cruelty. He rode with his hat tilted forward, the flesh around his eyes puckered to keep the raw ocean of sunlight away. He didn't get to the County Seat until shortly before sundown, put his horse up at a liverybarn and went to the Courthouse.

The sheriff was a big man with unnaturally thick lips, a wealth of gray hair and a petulant, immature look to his features. He exuded a sense of satisfaction at his own achievements. When Brandon entered the office he studied his face for a moment before he gestured toward a chair.

'Hot ride?'

Brandon said 'Yes,' and waited. The sheriff threw his bulk back in his chair. The swivel squeaked. He appeared to be arranging words.

'Brandy, that fence over at Fort Parker is a hot issue.'

Brandon still waited.

'I had four callers a couple of days ago about it. They said you were taking the part of the people who put the fence up. That right?'

'I haven't taken sides with anyone. That's not my job, taking sides.'

'Right,' the sheriff said with a brusque nod. 'Tell me – did you say to Jared Hoxey if he wanted anything done about that fence he'd have to do it himself?'

'I told Jared I wasn't going to tell the Grants to put gates in their fence. I don't have that power.'

'Ummmm.' The sheriff swiveled his chair half around and gazed out a window at the teeming town. 'Brandy, you know this girl pretty well?'

Brandon's fists closed slowly. 'I know her well enough,' he said evenly. 'I also knew her brother. He was bushwhacked last night. The doctor thinks he'll die.'

The sheriff's head came around. 'Bushwhacked?'

'Yeah. He was riding out by the fence and someone across it shot him off his horse.'

'Who did it?'

'I don't know yet. The kid's too badly hurt

to say, if he knows. It was pretty dark last night. I doubt if he saw the rawhider.'

The sheriff looked out the window again. Silence fell between them. The office seemed stifling to Brandon.

'Brandy; the cowmen asked me to send over a deputy from here. I can't, haven't got the men. I told them that and they asked me to appoint a man over there to fill the job.'

Brandon's breath went out of him slowly, not because of what the sheriff said – he'd expected Hoxey and the others to try and undermine him – but because the sheriff's tone indicated he thought the suggestion a good one.

'They gave me several names. Ed Spanner was one, Sam Morton was another – and Charley Belton.'

Brandon looked momentarily stricken. 'Belton's the man I gave my badge to this morning. He's going to watch things until I get back. The other two are rawhiders and cattlemen.'

'Yeah,' the sheriff said distantly. 'I know. Belton's all right though – you think?'

Brandon got up slowly. His stomach felt hollow and something hot and dry was burning behind his eyes. 'It looks to me,' he said, 'like you think I'm playing favorites. I don't know what Hoxey and the Spanners told you, Sheriff; I've played this straight.' He fished in his pants pocket, drew out his fist and threw something on the desk. 'If you'd take their word before you gave me a chance to talk, then you don't have enough confidence in me anyway. There's the deputy's badge. Give it to anyone you want to.'

He left the office without looking back. The sheriff watched him go with a half-angry, half-abashed expression.

Brandon got his horse and rode out of town into the lowering night. He pointed the black for Fort Parker and let him pick his own gait. The darkness was relieved by a skinny moon and a mass of tiny stars as clear-cut and shiny as new money.

He felt more indignation than anger. Five years as a deputy, as well as Town Marshal, and relieved like that. Politics: Hoxey was a big man in the country. With Wagonwheel, Spanners, and probably every other free-range cowman in the country behind him, maybe the sheriff had no choice. One deputy as opposed to big interests.

He made it back a couple of hours before sunup. Fort Parker was as still as a tomb. The faint light played over it with a gentleness that softened the square corners, the flaked paint, the harshness. The town looked actually pretty in the glowing pre-dawn. He dismounted at the lean-to, off-saddled, turned the black in with the grulla, forked over feed and went around to the office, dumped his hat on the desk and threw himself full length upon a cot back in the corner where the woodstove was.

Several hours later he was awakened by someone's spurs. Turning over, he saw Charley. He ran a hand through his hair and sat up, rubbed his eyes and stood up.

'By golly,' Charley said. 'You're loco to ride all day and all night too.'

'Not as loco as the sheriff,' Brandon said, pouring water into a washbasin, making masculine sounds when the coldness struck him, ran over his face and dripped off his chin. 'I got fired.' Charley didn't say anything. Brandon wiped on the roller-towel and peered behind some shaving equipment for a comb. 'Hoxey and some of the others went over there and sold the sheriff on firing me and hiring you or Ed Spanner or Sam Morton as new deputy.'

Charley still said nothing. When Brandon turned, Charley was sitting in the slat-bottomed chair with an unlit cigarette dangling from his mouth and an unstruck match in his right hand. Brandon combed back his hair, went around the desk and dropped down there. 'Give me your makings.' Charley dutifully tossed the sack and papers down. Brandon went to work on a cigarette. Charley finally spoke.

'Why me?'

Brandon shrugged without looking up. 'I don't know. The sheriff said your name. You and Ed and Sam.' He lit and exhaled and stared at Charley. 'All cowmen, naturally.'

Charley took a long drag of his cigarette and contemplated the tip of it in silence. After a moment, he said: 'Not me, Brandy. I wouldn't touch that job with a prod-pole.'

'You should though, Charley. Listen: if you don't take it Ed or Sam Morton will. You know what'll happen then, don't you?'

'Yeah; no fence.' Charley used his little finger to flick off ash. 'And, if I *did* take it I'd be in the same spot you're in, only worse. I'm a cowman – a little one, sure – but still a cowman. If I did anything to hold the others back – you know what'd happen to me?' Charley looked steadily at Brandon. 'They'd gut-shoot my cows and burn my cabin. Nothing doing. No thanks, Brandy. Let 'em appoint Ed or Sam. I don't want any part of it. Nossir.'

'Well,' Brandon said, 'they'll appoint *somebody,* Charley, and you can bet your boots it'll be a cowman.'

'And you? What're you going to do?'

Brandon looked frowningly at his cigarette. Irrelevantly he said: 'I don't see how people smoke these things before breakfast.' He smashed the cigarette against the underside of his desk and tossed it into the spittoon. 'Me? I gave the sheriff back my deputy's badge. In an hour or so I'm going over and give the town fathers my marshal's badge.'

'Thought it all out, huh?'

'Thought it all out on the way back here last night. As Town Marshal I've got no authority beyond town. Well – the war's on Charley, and whether I wanted it like this or not I'm in it up to my ears, so I might just as well get all the way in.'

'You mean go out there and work for her?'

'Yes.'

Charley looked strained and worried. He gazed at his cigarette again, thoughtfully. 'Isn't there another way, Brandy?'

'I can't see it and I've looked at the thing from all angles since I left the sheriff's office last night. They got my deputy's badge, that means I'm hamstrung outside of town. In town, there won't be any way I can stop what's coming or make anyone see what this'll lead to. Well, Charley, that puts it squarely up to me whether I'm going to hang around town arresting a drunk now and then while they're trying to ride over her rough-shod or whether I jump in on her side.'

Charley tossed his cigarette away and stood up. 'Let's get something to eat. I'm not exactly hungry right now, but I can think better when I can smell coffee.' He reached up and unconsciously pulled his hat forward, over his eyes, and watched Brandon arise, don his hat and walk around the desk. 'I'd hate to see Ed Spanner as a deputy sheriff,' he said slowly. 'He's always been kind of overbearing, ever since I can remember.'

Brandon swung back the door. 'Then you'd better take it. But, Charley, if you do – well – you and I, we'd–'

'Yeah,' Charley said dryly, passing through the opening out into the dazzling early morning light. 'Like I said before, I wouldn't touch it with a prod-pole.' They crossed the road before Charley spoke again. 'Sam Morton might not be too bad.'

Brandon pushed through the Drover's restaurant door and said: 'Remember the size of the feller that shot Milt?'

Charley went ahead to the table and sat down, rolled one fist inside the other and looked at his knuckles. 'I can't picture Sam being a bushwhacker. Hell, he isn't the type.'

'Neither is Jared Hoxey, Charley, but I'll give you odds Sam Morton or Jared shot that kid.'

Charley shook his head. 'Won't bet you,' he said, 'but I don't believe either of them did it. It'd be a hired job, Brandy.'

'Nope. No strangers in town and, whoever did it had no idea the kid was coming along. They were out there to cut the fence, *I* think, and he stumbled onto them. It wasn't planned. I can see that now. How would anyone know the kid was going to take a notion to ride out there?'

Charley shook his head and didn't answer. When the waiter came up Brandon ordered beef and eggs for them both, and black coffee, then he looked at Charley's anxious features. 'How is Milt, by the way?'

'Fair. I talked to the doc last night in the saloon. He said the kid was coming along a lot better'n he had any right to.'

'You didn't go out?'

'No,' Charley said, settling back, looking tiredly around the room. 'I reckon I just plain didn't have the guts to, Brandy. She took all the spook out of me the other night. I don't think I could stand seeing her like that again.'

'Thanks to the cowmen,' Brandon said.

Charley's eyes swung and settled on Brandon's face. He didn't say anything. The food came. They ate in silence, drank their coffee and Charley made another cigarette. 'I can't do it,' he said out of a clear sky.

Brandon looked over at him. 'Do what?'

'Take the deputy's job. Brandy, I've never been in such a spot in my life.'

Brandon tossed a silver dollar on the table. He was thinking of the way he'd seen Charley look at Marti, when he got up and reached for his hat, and a thought occurred to him that made him feel a lot better.

'Me, too. You know, Charley, if he hadn't sort of asked for my badge I'd have quit anyway. I didn't see that until right now, but I would have. Hell; a man couldn't sit by and watch them go after her like they're going to – could he?'

'No.'

Brandon took the marshal's badge back from Charley and left him on the plankwalk outside the Drover's. He went down to the little building beside the blacksmith's shop where the town fathers, elected councilmen, met and banged on the door. He knew there wouldn't be anyone there but he knocked anyway. The building sent back a ghostly echo. He went into the smithy and was greeted by a powerfully built man with a habit of lowering his head and peering over his spectacles; the blacksmith, who was also, by right of continuous service, Senior Councilman. Brandon held out his closed fist. The smith put out his hand with a twinkle in his eye.

'Jokes so early in the day,' he said. Then, when the dull circlet with the star in its center lay in his hand, its meaning sinking in slowly, the blacksmith's head came up, the smile was gone. 'What are you doing, Brandy?'

'Quitting. The sheriff sort of fired me yesterday over the Grant fence. If he doesn't want me I don't think you fellers should keep me either.' He started to turn away.

'Wait a minute,' the blacksmith said in a crackling voice. 'Just a damned minute, Brandy. *We* tell the sheriff who we want as deputy over here; he don't tell *us*.'

'This time he's going to. He's going to

appoint Sam Morton or Ed Spanner or Charley Belton in my place. You'll hear about it in a day or so.'

The blacksmith's face grew dark. 'As long as Fort Parker pays half the wages of the deputy over here, by God it'll be Fort Parker says who the deputy is.' He pushed the badge back toward Brandon. 'You take this, Brandy. One of us'll ride over there and see old possum-belly to-day. He'll not dictate to this town.'

Brandon shook his head, looking at the callused hand and the dully shining badge in it. 'Sorry.'

He walked out of the shop knowing the blacksmith was still standing like a statue, his hard face getting harder looking.

He went to his office, cleaned out the desk, took all his personal effects to his room over the Drover's and went back, saddled the grulla horse and led the black one and rode northwest out of town.

The day was cowed under the heat-lash. Riding over the range as far as the stage road would take him to the Grant place; he looked for signs of life. The first he saw was when he'd passed the turn-off to the Grant ranch and there, just outside the new fence, lying close enough to see the brands, were some cattle.

Out of idle curiosity he rode close enough to read brands. It was a mixed bunch; there were three animals with bows branded upon their ribs, one big four-year-old steer with a wagonwheel showing dark against the sun-burnt lightness of his summer hair, and a cow and calf with JEF on the right hip, for the Spanners. He smiled at them when they jumped up, watching him.

'Waiting to get through, are you?' he said aloud. 'I'll give you odds you don't.'

Chapter Four

For a number of reasons Brandon's heart was pumping solidly when he stepped down in front of the Grant house and went up to the door, rolled his knuckles over it softly and waited, his hat dangling from one hand.

Marti appeared in the opening dry-eyed, which surprised him, and with a shiny nose and an unnatural cant to her jaw. Her eyes lit up at sight of him. She smiled, which surprised him even more, and moved back.

'Coffee's on, Marshal.'

He walked softly, wincing when a board squeaked under his weight. She had on another of those dresses that flared from the waist down and fit closely from the waist up, only this one had a square, low neckline.

'How's Milt?'

'You won't believe it,' she said, swinging towards the stove. 'He was lying there with his eyes open when I went in this morning. Lord you just can't know. Brandy...' She caught her underlip between her teeth and poured two cups of coffee. He looked for and found, her eyelashes. After she'd put the pot back she looked up at him. Her eyes had the dark shadows back in them. 'He smiled at me but he looks awful.'

'Did he say anything?'

She sat down across from him and put cream and sugar in her coffee. 'No. I didn't give him a chance to. I patted his face and made him some broth. He ate it – drank it, rather. After that I had to look after the baby. I haven't been back in there since.' She looked up again with a sparkling smile that made her nose wrinkle where the freckles were. 'Isn't that wonderful?'

'Yes.'

She studied him for a moment. A shadow passed over her face. 'Brandy. Regrets?'

He didn't understand right away. They looked at one another for a moment, then he felt the blood coursing under his cheeks. 'No'm. No regrets. I never will have 'em – if you're thinking what I'm thinking.'

'I am.'

He backed up to safer ground. 'Well – would you be interested in hiring a rider, ma'm? That's what I rode out here to ask you.' He told her about the sheriff, about handing in his Town Marshal's badge. She stirred her coffee without seeming to be aware she was doing it until he finished, then she laid the spoon aside and said:

'You shouldn't have, Brandy. The fence isn't that important.'

He raised his eyebrows. 'Isn't it? Your brother came within an ace of getting killed over the fence.'

'No one knows that better than I do. If I'd known what it would cause I never would have mentioned a fence.'

'I told you they wouldn't like it. Anyway, that's water under the dam. You've made it and you've got to back it up.'

'Why?'

He blinked. 'Why? Why – because you built it. Folks don't do things without meaning to do them, Marti. You've made a fence and you've got to make it stand. Folks don't cut and run the first time someone snarls at them over something they've done.'

'Milt's life and your future is much more important than that fence.'

He felt lost, adrift, so he dropped his eyes to the coffee, watched the steam rising around the outer edges of the cup, lifted it and sipped. She got up, went around the table and put her hand on his shoulder. It was like having a fire burst out inside him when she touched him.

101

'Brandy; let's forget the fence.'

He remained silent, feeling the strangeness within.

'I shouldn't have tried to change things, only it seemed like a much better idea, much more scientific and sensible to run cattle like that. But I don't want to fight, Brandy. I really don't.'

He twisted around so he could look at her. 'You *can't* make a play and not back it up. Folks just don't do things like that.'

'Maybe men don't,' she said, 'but I'm not a man.'

'No one'd ever make that mistake,' he said, before he knew how it sounded, then he plunged on eager to drown out its echo. 'You've got the fence and you've got to make them respect it.'

'Do I?' She was watching him closely.

'Yes.'

'All right. I'll have to hire you then, won't I, because even if Milt could do the fighting, I don't think he'd be able to. Westerners are – savage – aren't they?'

He stood up and her hand fell off his shoulder. They weren't more than six inches apart. A thick vein in the side of his neck pulsed and she moved away without seeming to.

'Let's go see if Milt can talk.'

When they entered his room Milton's eyes moved and that was all. Brandon thought he looked even less alive than he had the night of the shooting, if that was possible. His shape under the bedclothes was emaciated looking, flat and bony. He nodded at the youth and sat upon a little bench beside the bed.

'Can you talk, Milt?'

The answer was just a trifle stronger than a whisper. 'I guess. He sure got me, didn't he?'

'Yeah. Who was he?'

'Don't know. Ridin' along – that's all I remember. In bed here, next.'

'You didn't see anything? Hear a horse – anything Milt?'

'Nothing. Didn't even hear his gun.'

Brandon got up and nodded down at the boy. He didn't know whether he really expected anything different or not, but he knew real disappointment just the same. 'Well; get some rest.'

He went out of the room and back to the kitchen, poured himself another cup of coffee and turned when Marti came back. She looked happy.

'He wants some more broth.'

'Good.' He watched her make it and drank the coffee, set the cup down and reached for his hat. 'Can I put my gatherings in the bunkhouse?'

She looked at him blankly. 'Oh – yes. You won't be crowded. There's only Cal left.'

'Cal?'

'The cowboy we inherited with the ranch,'

she said lightly. 'The others quit.'

He could have groaned. Two men and a girl couldn't begin to do what would have to be done.

He led both horses to the corrals and turned them in, hunted up the hayfork and fed them, climbed over the rails and lugged his saddle into the barn, hung it up by one stirrup and unlashed the saddlebags, threw them over his shoulder and hiked toward the bunkhouse. The dead-eyed cowboy was watching him from the doorway, a stub of a cigarette in his fingers.

'Howdy.'

Brandon brushed past him. 'Howdy. Which is your bunk?' The man pointed to a lower one close by the door and Brandon took the opposite one, dumped the saddle-bags on it and thumbed back his hat. It was hot. 'I'll be riding here for a while,' he said, looking into the tightness of the older man's face. 'My name's Brandon Parker.'

'I know. Town Marshal. My name's Cal Stephans.'

'Yeah. Well, I'm a Grant rider now, Cal, not Town Marshal.' He saw the eyes widen slightly. 'Sort of half-quit, half got fired.'

Cal grunted with elaborate casualness and walked as far as the table in the middle of the room, straddled the bench and punched out his cigarette. 'Regular hired hand?'

'That's right.'

Cal smiled expansively. 'I'm glad of that. We got some fence work to do today and I been tellin' myself all kinds of lies to keep from goin' out there.'

'What kind of fence work?'

'Mending. We had visitors a night or so back. She's cut in about five places.'

Brandon sighed. 'Well, let's get started. I'm kind of soft,' he added, absently, staring at the floor. 'I don't expect you have any ideas about who cut it?'

Cal stood up and wagged his head. 'Nary a one. Or should I say I got ten ideas an' no way to know which one is right?'

They went out back into the smashing sunlight. Cal brought in a team of big seal-browns. They harnessed them in silence. Cal took the lines and jerked his head at the bed of the wagon.

'Everything we need's in there.'

They went straight toward the fence, due north. The wagon jolted and groaned every inch of the way. It was more than an hour later that they saw the shining strands. Cal lined the team out eastward and spoke around a plug of tobacco he was gnawing at.

'Best to go right up to the first one and work back.' He offered the plug, got a negative headshake and pocketed it. 'I got an idea the Grants're going to have to hire a man just to ride this cussed fence. If we was patching five miles down the line, cowmen could be up here cutting it.' He looked at Brandon with a sardonic twinkle. 'Nice thought, ain't it?'

Brandon didn't answer. Up ahead he saw the broken strands. Fortunately, since the posts were only twenty-five feet apart and set two feet deep into the ground, when one section of wire was cut the rest of the wires on both sides stayed taut.

When Cal Stephans set the foot-brake and looped the lines, Brandon leapt down and drew on his gloves. A totally foreign wrath was growing inside him. He had no use for barbed-wire, but he was standing *inside* a fence now, not outside of it. It made a personal difference.

Marti's cowboy knew how to splice wire. Brandon learned by watching. They mended the break and turned the wagon westward. Cal shifted his cud to speak.

'It's sort of useless, ain't it?'

'That's what I've been thinking. We can go on mending this thing every couple of days and whoever's cutting it can slip back in the night and break it in a new place. After a while there'll be nothing but patches. Seven miles of them.'

'That's what I know. I got an idea this morning. Set wolf traps.'

Brandon rode hunched over until they came to the next break. When the wagon stopped he climbed down. 'Stay here a minute, Cal,' he said, and walked through the broken strands.

The ground was like iron. A scant quarter inch of dust lay over it. He found smudges but no tracks worth the name. Cal called out to him: 'Wastin' your time, Marshal. I've tried that, too. Wrong time of the year to read much off the ground.'

They went about repairing the break. When Cal was lifting the lines to drive on, Brandon leapt up beside him. 'That wolf trap idea isn't all bad, Cal.'

'No,' the cowboy said. 'Thing is, you'd have to hide the marks pretty well and you'd have to plant 'em all around. It'd take time.'

Brandon squinted down the fence. 'I think we'll have lots for that,' he said. 'They cut at night, we patch up by day. Time won't mean much.'

He drank out of the burlap-covered jug and set it back in the shade under the seat. 'Getting enough traps in Fort Parker to do us any good will be just about impossible. The word would get around that Grant ranch bought wolf traps. The rawhiders wouldn't be long figuring that out.'

'Sounds right,' Cal said. 'We could send to Denver for 'em.'

Brandon was slow replying. He'd seen the third break and inside it, spread out and eating greedily were Bow cattle. Cal swore.

When the wagon got to the break they climbed down. Cal squinted dourly at the animals.

'Got to go back now, get horses, come back and drive 'em out.'

'How about the team?' Brandon asked. 'Saddlebroke?'

Cal's face brightened a little. 'Well; I've ridden 'em to and from. They aren't cutting horses by a damned sight but it might work, save riding three miles and back. We could try it.'

They did; took the horses off the tongue, looped the traces and clambered upon their broad backs, got the cattle rounded up and eased through the fence. Cal laughed loud and exultantly when they were hitching up again.

'That'll show 'em, by God.'

They worked until the sun was setting, until every break was mended, and by then Brandon's anger was cold and still. He didn't say five words all the way back to the ranch. Cal, taking his cue from the younger, larger man, lapsed into a silence of his own.

Brandon washed up at the stand behind the bunkhouse where a hand-pump was. He stood in the evening shade letting the heat finish drying his face and hair while Cal sluiced off. Blowing like a half-drowned bull the cowboy flicked off water, groped for the dirty towel hanging from a nearby nail. Cal was trying to say something through the cloth when a cow bell clanged around in front.

'Supper, Marshal.'

They went across the yard and Marti met them. She looked at Brandon's red face, chapped lips and punctured shirt. The soft twinkle in her eyes died out when she saw his face. Bleak and inward looking, grimly withdrawn. She made conversation while they ate and Cal answered every time she spoke. Brandon thought a little sardonically that it wasn't just Marti's cooking that kept the grizzled old cowhand on the ranch.

When the meal was over Cal arose with a funny little grin. 'Never got used to smokin' inside,' he said. 'Been raised for too many years the other way.' He went toward the door leading to the veranda with his tobacco sack dangling from his fingers.

Brandon got up too. Marti frowned just the slightest bit at him. 'Are you *sure* you have no regrets, Brandy? You don't act like you did the night of the dance.'

He gazed down at her. The look of uncertainty, half-ashamed, on her face made the funny feeling come back. He went around the table without answering, reached down and tilted her head back, leaned low and kissed her. She responded with ardor and he straightened up suddenly and ran a finger over the saddle of her nose where the freckles were.

'I told you: I'm not sorry and I never will be. You're the best thing that could happen to a man – to me.' A twinge of memory showed him Charley Belton's averted face at the Drover's. The way Charley had used those words about her.

'Brandy...'

'Marti, I've got an idea. Cal and I may not be around the house tonight. All right?'

She stood up close to him, no bigger than a minute. 'Brandy – don't do anything reckless, will you?'

He touched her hair and went back around the table and outside. Cal was sitting on the stoop. Smoke drifted lazily up past his far-seeing eyes. The land was mauve and still in a brooding way. At eventide it had the strong dry-grass-and-sage scent that seemed to come up out of the earth itself. Cow-country smell.

'Cal, do you think they might come back tonight?'

The cowboy shrugged, exhaled smoke. 'I wouldn't bet either way,' he said, 'but if they knew we'd fixed that fence I expect they'd whack it again.' He looked around at Brandon with his dead-looking eyes. 'Do you get the creeps out there? I do. Feel like fellers're watching me from the hills around. Same sort of feelin' I used to get when there was Indians slipping around. Oldtimers used to call it "smelling Indians". Same sort of a feeling.'

'Well,' Brandon said thoughtfully, 'we can't get the wolf traps in time to scare them away, I'm convinced of that now. Maybe we ought to do something else.'

The dead-alive eyes never flickered. 'You got an idea?'

'Just the makings of one. Suppose you were to ride east, over toward the stage road where the fence ends, and get up on a slope over there that's close to the road. I saw such a place when I rode in here. There's a little seepage-spring near it. Some cattle were lyin' around there.'

'I know the spot. What then?'

'Ride up there close to the fence, Cal. If they're coming from Bow and Spanner and Wagonwheel they'll be riding from the east. You'd see them, maybe. Let them get a mile or so along the fence then light a match 'way back behind them.'

'Oh,' Cal said, with a dawning look of comprehension. 'And you'll be about where the critters were today, watching for the light?'

'That's right. Think it'll work?'

Cal ruminated. 'Well – if it did it'd mean we wouldn't have to mess with that damned barbed wire tomorrow, wouldn't it?'

'Game?'

'I reckon.'

They sat a while longer, then Brandon

stood up, goaded by impatience. Cal let off the faintest of sighs and stomped on his cigarette. 'We'd best take a blanket apiece,' he said, 'just in case they don't come.' He started to move toward the bunkhouse then stopped and gestured backwards toward the house with his head. 'What about her? You going to tell her?'

'I told her we might not be around tonight.'

Cal nodded and started off. Brandon followed him. They each rolled a blanket, saddled up and tied the bedrolls behind their cantles, mounted and rode out of the yard southerly. A half mile or so from the house Brandon reined up.

'We'd better split up here, Cal. Don't forget the match. I'll be watching.'

Cal rode due east and Brandon plodded southeastward. The night was down with a ghostly light from a sickle moon making the range watered-milk white. There wasn't a sound. It was like riding through time all the way to the fenceline and there, with pale silver gleamings east and west, stood the barbed barrier with its soldier ranks of posts.

Brandon sat his horse a moment looking at the fence, then he turned and rode eastward as far as a knoll he had in his mind's eye. After that there was the waiting. A time when he took his thoughts down and examined them and wished he knew who he might be fighting. Cattlemen, yes, but which ones?

In his mind was a faceless phantom about five inches shorter than he was who rode a bay horse, wore old boots and fired a .30.30 with an off-center firing pin. Hoxey? It didn't seem reasonable. Fat Spanner? It could be Fat but he had never impressed Brandon as the kind of man, still – that was the hell of it; you couldn't tell.

He got wearily off his horse and stood beside it listening to the waves of silence that lay in layers over the range. After a while he hunkered, facing the east, hat back, the benign coolness engulfing him. Then it became difficult to stay awake, so he moved every little while and fought a lethargic battle with the night, batted his eyes and told himself if they didn't come he and Cal would sleep the next day and resume their vigil the following night: they'd come sometime.

Once he thought he heard a singing tremor in the distance. The kind of a noise the fence would make if it were cut, but there was no repetition while he hunkered, tense and abruptly wide awake; no match flare eastward. The hours passed and finally with a shrug he stood up and stretched. Off on the horizon the faintest of dawn-banners hung spectrally over the drowsy world. He mounted and struck out eastward to meet Cal. They weren't coming after all.

He rode a full two miles before he saw the

first cut. After that, the farther he rode the more breaks he passed. By the time daylight was bursting over the rim of the world he lifted his horse into a smooth lope and held him to it until he saw the head-down horse riderless, in the distance.

Cal was lying on the ground with both eyes open and bloodshot. He didn't speak until Brandon swung down and knelt beside him, then he rolled over and held up his arms. They were bound viciously tight at the wrists with blood-slippery wraps of barbed wire.

Brandon's horror at the sight of the shredded wrists made him stiffen a moment before he went to work. When the last strand was unwound, Cal's arms freed, the cowboy sat there looking at the dripping blood without any particular expression. Finally he sighed and made as though to rise. Brandon helped him.

'No sense askin' Marshal, because I never seen 'em. Must have spied me on the skyline slipped up and busted me over the head from behind. Hell of a note. I didn't even hear anything. Like Indians.'

'Forget it for now,' Brandon said. 'We'll get back to the ranch. Do they hurt?'

Cal wriggled his fingers a little. 'No. Circulation must've stopped while I was knocked out. They're beginning to tingle a little now. Sure a mess, aren't they?'

Brandon brought Cal's horse closer and helped him to mount it. He watched to see if the bleeding was excessive. It didn't appear to be, just big, black-looking drops falling onto his soggy pants now and then. It made Brandon's scalp crawl, watching.

'Make me a cigarette, will you, Marshal?'

Brandon reined over close, fished the tobacco sack out of Cal's jumper and twisted up a smoke, lit it and stuck it into the shorter man's mouth. Cal inhaled deeply, exhaled, made a sickly smile. 'Great stuff,' he said. 'Did you see anything?'

'No, but a little before dawn I thought I heard wires giving away.'

'Must of been them.'

Brandon herded Cal around in back of the bunkhouse when they got back to the ranch. Once he raised his head to listen. There wasn't a sound anywhere. He put up the horses and went to the washstand behind the bunkhouse with Cal. The cowboy swore with vigor when the water gushed over his mangled flesh. By the time Brandon had smeared his wrists with sweet-oil and wrapped them in bandages his facial contortions had stopped. He even raised his whiskery face once and smiled at Brandon.

'You know, I don't think I ever heard of anyone being tied up with barbed wire before. Of course the first one'd have to be me, 'cause I just naturally hate the stuff.'

'Stay here a while,' Brandon said, arising. 'I'll go see if there's a chance for us to get something to eat.'

'Sure.' Cal watched Brandon cross the yard with a peculiarly tight-looking smile wreathing his face. He gave one shake of his head.

When Brandon stepped onto the porch, spurs ringing, Marti threw the door open. Her nostrils quivered. 'You're a sight,' she said in a small voice, looking at something he hadn't noticed. Cal's blood on his shirt. He went past her into the house. She hadn't been up very long, but the stove was crackling.

'Marti, will you fix Cal some breakfast? Somebody clouted him over the head last night and tied his arms with barbed wire. Don't look so scairt, he'll be all right, but right now he needs some warm food.'

'Where is he, Brandy?'

'I left him over at the bunkhouse because I wanted to talk to you alone for a minute.'

'Does he need the doctor?'

Brandon shook his head. 'No, but he won't be able to do anything for a week or so. Listen, Marti – I've been thinking. We can't do this alone. You and Cal and I aren't enough. I reckon I'd better ride over to Fillmore, that's the County Seat. It may take me a day or so.' He smiled down at her; there were deep circles drawn low under his eyes. 'I've got an idea. I hope this one pans out better'n the one last night did.'

'Brandy–'

'Don't worry. You've got plenty to do. The baby, Milt, and now Cal.'

Without any warning she threw both her arms around him and pushed her face against his chest. Indistinctly she said, 'Brandy, be careful.'

He put his cheek down against her hair and stood motionless for a moment, then carefully removed her arms and put two fingers under her chin and kissed her.

She watched him from the doorway as he re-crossed the yard to the bunkhouse. There was a cloudy look to her gaze and something she had never allowed him to see, was there. Fear.

He pushed back the door and rocked his head at Cal. 'She's up. Go on over, Cal. And – I'll be gone for a spell, so you'd best stick close to the house.' He looked pointedly at a Winchester carbine in a saddleboot leaning in a corner. 'Keep your eyes peeled. S'long.'

The prospect of riding forty miles in the blasting sunlight wasn't pleasant. Neither was the ordeal of doing it, but he used the grulla horse, as tough as jerky, and by evening he was nearing the outskirts of Fillmore. It wasn't until he was among the horsemen and buggies and saw people looking at him in a strange way that he remembered he hadn't shaved nor slept and must look pretty awful.

In a tonsorial parlor he got a shave and a much needed bath, but his eyes felt like there was sand under the lids even after the last light died and twilight came. By then he was making the rounds of the saloons. What he had in mind was simple enough. He needed help; hard men. Before the fall round-up began there were always riders hanging around the towns. Hiring men to fight wasn't hard, it was the fighting wages they demanded that hurt. He hired four hard-looking cowboys for one week for as much as they'd make in a month of normal cowboying, told them to meet him at the liverybarn the following morning at dawn, then crawled into the hay near his horse and slept like a stone.

On the road back, in the fresh early light he thought of the cattlemen he was going to face and drew some satisfaction from the fact that the four men riding with him looked like the kind who would spit in the devil's eye. They were, he knew, not only tough, but anxious to prove they were tougher. One, a swarthy, stocky man with an ivory-butted six-gun, was called Emory; the others were just names and faces, a little disreputable, a little reckless, and willing to fight anybody on earth just for the hell of it.

The conversation throughout the day on the way back was about fences in general, which none of them liked, and about moneyed cowmen who shot kids and intimidated their sisters. Brandon let the riders think Milt was younger than he was. He did nothing to give them reason to believe the cowmen might have any right on their side. He did it deliberately and calculatingly; if Hoxey and the Spanners wanted a fence war, they were going to get it. Anything Brandon could think of to further the Grants' cause, he told his hirelings, and within him there grew a savage satisfaction. Someone was going to be damned sorry they tied Cal's wrists with that barbed wire.

That evening, when they were back, their horses turned out and fed and the men snugged up around Marti's kitchen table, Brandon saw that he had overlooked something. The men were in silent raptures over Marti. When the uncomfortable meal was over and the men had trooped outside to smoke, Brandon lingered in the kitchen. Marti gazed up at him.

'What on earth are you going to do with *them*, Brandy? I never saw such a – a–'

'How're Milt and Cal?'

She kept her lips poised over the word she never uttered, looking at him, then she smiled in a slow and tantalizing way and put her arms behind her on the table. 'You're such a strange person, Brandy. Maybe it's best that you are.'

'I don't know what you mean,' he said,

quite honestly.

She leaned back. 'Ten years from now you'll know. I think you'll understand by then.'

'That doesn't sound very complimentary, Marti.'

'It wasn't. I'm sorry. Brandy, why did you bring those men back with you? We don't need cowboys just yet, do we?'

'No – not cowboys. What happened to Cal isn't going to happen again. It's your turn now; the cowmen've had their licks.'

'Of course, it's the fence, isn't it?'

'Yes. Cal told you what happened, didn't he?'

'Yes. He doesn't seem to know much except that someone hit him on the head, though.'

'That's what I mean, Marti. Any hitting from now on Grant ranch is going to do it. I hope it'll be tonight.'

'You haven't had any rest. Can't you wait until some other night?'

He gazed at her blankly for a moment, then he smiled. 'Golly; I'm not sure I'll ever understand *you*, Marti.'

'We're not as far apart as you think.' She drew in a shallow breath. 'Brandy – what's it like to be in love?'

He got beet-red and made a funny sound in his throat and said: 'I'll see you in the morning, Marti.'

The four riders had to have fresh horses. So did Brandon. Cal was at the corral gawking when they finally finished roping ranch animals and re-saddling. Every man but Brandon had a carbine in a saddleboot, butt forward and tilted up. As Brandon went by Cal touched his knee.

'I could hold the horses, Marshal.'

'I've got a better job for you. Is there a plow around the ranch?'

Cal looked startled. 'A plow? You mean a walking plow like "grangers use?"'

'Yes.'

'There's an old one in the blacksmith's shop, but there's no trees to it.'

'Rig it up, Cal. We're going to do some plowing tomorrow.' He reined away and left Cal standing behind like a bent stick of wood, looking after them.

On fresh horses the four riders seemed to absorb animal energy through the seat of their pants. Two smoked and one hummed a ribald song, while the fourth, a dark-eyed, swarthy man, edged closer to Brandon on the right side. His handsome ivory-butted gun was lashed tightly to his leg.

'Parker; you paying a bounty by any chance?'

Brandon looked into the dark face and shook his head. 'No. I don't want any killing unless we have to, but I'll give fifty dollars a head, for every fence-cutter you take alive.'

The dark man patted his lariat and called to the others. 'Fifty dollars a head alive, fellers.' The others swore happily. Brandon listened and hoped with every shred of his being the cowmen would come tonight to cut the fence.

Brandon dropped the men off on little knolls that ran westward from the stage road. He cautioned each man of the danger of being bushwhacked like Milt and Cal had been, explained how to signal with the flare of a match, then he rode eastward, by himself until he was upon the little knoll where Cal had been downed.

He hobbled his horse with the sky backgrounding him and moved a hundred feet farther eastward afoot, over where the fence was. Beyond, in the silvery light and not far off, he could see the stage road.

Like before, the night was moonwashed and as still, as deeply brooding as it could be. He lay full length in the grass with his head on his hands, thinking. If it weren't for Marti he wouldn't be there and while he didn't like the idea of a fence any better than the next man, still, he believed in her right to build a fence on her own land. Felt strongly about it and thought that, perhaps, even if it hadn't been her fence, he'd have felt the same way. Cussed cowmen'd had it all their own way long enough, riding roughshod over anyone who stood up and faced them. Maybe's he'd been getting antagonistic to them for a long time. He shrugged and let his eyes sweep the wide perimeter of the low horizon. A faint iridescence hugged the ground.

He'd seen the cowmen do other things that stuck in his craw. He understood why they had done them, knew that cowman-gun-law had been their way of life too long for them to accept or employ any other kind. Well, bred to the saddle or not he'd had enough. If it hadn't been Marti it would have been someone else, maybe. He looked up at the sky. Not as pretty and kind of helpless, little and with cornflower colored eyes, a strong mouth that was full and mobile and up-curling. He moved restlessly on the ground. The hours dragged by.

It would cost him half of what he'd saved as Town Marshal to pay off his toughs, but it might be worth it; would be worth it if he got one good chance at the fencecutters. He thought of Jared Hoxey and Fat Spanner. Even of Sam Morton of Wagonwheel. Seemed kind of strange after knowing them so long to be – literally – across a fence from them. Somewhere, eastward, it sounded like, he heard a steel shoe strike a rock.

He raised only his head out of the grass, tense, straining, but the sound didn't come again. Waiting, he became aware of little rustling sounds around him. Field mice, nocturnal animals out foraging. He looked up at his horse on the knoll, watched it closely, but the animal was head-down drowsing. If there were horsemen out there the animal hadn't heard or scented them yet.

A long way off, southward, a cow bellowed. The sound came so softly it might have been the sighing of the wind. If there'd been any wind. He tilted his head and wondered if the cow, too, heard men, or whether she was just anxious about a calf who had wandered out of sight. He studied the horizon again, taking lots of time. There was nothing to see, no sound.

His attention was drawn to the knoll where his horse snorted softly. The animal had its head up now, ears forward, looking south. Fine. With a thudding heart, Brandon unshipped his hand-gun and waited. Something out there; it might be animals, but it also might be men.

A little later he thought he heard a solid rumbling noise but wasn't sure. It might have come out of the ground he was lying on. He got to one knee still holding the gun. No, he hadn't felt it, he'd heard it. Standing erect, tingling, he cocked his head. There was no mistaking the rattle, the drumming insistence; cattle. He looked anxiously up at his horse, purposefully left up there so a watcher could skyline him, try to ambush Brandon like Cal had been ambushed. The beast was staring straight out into the night, but downward, a little, as tense as a coiled spring. Brandon swore. That *had* been a rider he'd heard a half hour or so before, and he'd bet fifty dollars the cowmen had sent him up to watch Brandon's silhouetted mount. Brandon's bait had backfired. He could imagine the rawhider lying in the grass beyond the fence, waiting. If Brandon went up to his horse he'd get what Milt got. Dammit! He studied the direction the horse was staring in. The land was eerily opalescent, the drumroll of hooves was getting louder.

They were driving a herd ahead of them. They'd *virile* them right through the fence and if Brandon tried to get ahorseback to turn them...

He acted on impulse. Running quickly eastward he made a big circle. Several hundred yards down the fence he trotted south, toward the wire. He didn't climb through the fence, but slid under it, lay for a long time listening and looking, then got up and struck out southward again, lungs pumping like a blacksmith's bellows. Well below where he thought he'd heard the horseshoe strike rock, he began an angling course back up toward the fence. That was when he heard the wires give with a singing whine. Immediately the pained, angry bellows of cattle arose into the electric tension that seemed to live in the night.

They were through.

He was perspiring as though it was broad daylight, running in a tired, grim jag with the night air stinging his throat like creosote. The riders would be off to his right somewhere, but if there was a rawhider lying up near the fence somewhere watching Brandon's horse he'd have to be directly ahead.

But he wasn't and Brandon knew it when he saw the fence twenty feet ahead of him. Daylight would show whether there had been one or not. If there had been he'd mounted up and ridden away as soon as the cattle were through the fence.

Brandon stopped beside the fence and stood motionless, head up. There was only the sound of cows whose calves were lost in the night. No man-sounds, no running horses he could detect over the noise of the cattle, no shouts. Anger coursed through him like whiskey, made his mind hear and see things through a red haze. He climbed through the fence and stalked back to his horse with the knowledge of his second defeat very large within him. He mounted recklessly and rode westward. Almost immediately he began to see cattle. They were spooky. When his horse loomed up in the darkness they would throw up their heads, snort and run. To hell with them.

He rode a long time. In fact, the first rays of the new day were slanting down across the range before he and his four riders were together again. By then his anger was deep enough to mar the usually good-natured expression of his face.

He picked out three of the men and grunted at them. 'We'll round 'em up and push 'em back through the holes they made.'

The fourth man, he of the dark eyes and ivory-butted gun, scowled. 'What about me?'

Brandon said: 'You go back to the ranch and get Cal to help you harness the team to the wagon. It's got fence fixing stuff in it. Drive it back out here and we'll patch things up.'

He was riding east again, silent men on both sides of him, when one of them said, 'I thought I heard cattle. Put my ear to the ground. They sounded a hell of a way on, though.'

'They were. Up where I was, not far from the stage road. I didn't have a chance to signal to you fellers. There,' Brandon flung out his arm, 'you can see them spreading out.'

Someone swore. 'Lot of 'em. Pushed 'em through the fence, did they? I'll be damned – whoever done that must've been bunching 'em all evenin' to get that many rounded up.'

'Naw,' another rider said. 'All a feller have to do in this country if he wanted a herd'd be ride up a creek somewhere. As hot's it is now critters'd hang around the willow-breaks.'

Brandon gazed at the man, but said nothing. That had been spoken like an experienced cowman – or a rustler.

They fanned out and began pushing the cattle back toward the broken places in the fence. It wasn't hard to do, the animals had been eating without let-up since they'd come through the fence. They were logy.

When the last animal was back beyond the fence, Brandon dismounted and gazed up and down the intervals between the posts. The vein in the side of his neck was throbbing. Two of the riders sat in the shade of their horses and began to make cigarettes. The third man was gazing at the feed on both sides of the fence. He glanced over at Brandon.

'I got no use for fences. Never thought I'd see the day I'd hire out to protect one, but by God, look at the difference in the feed.'

Brandon nodded without speaking. The rider hitched up his pants and spat. 'Might be something to these things at that,' he said. 'I'm an open-minded feller. Don't believe a person ought to stick to something just because it's it.'

'A fence,' Brandon said sharply, 'isn't any better than the people who own it, in this kind of country. If they don't protect it it's nothing but a waste of money.'

The rider was still looking at the stands of feed. 'Feed's ten times better on this side than it is over there. That's good enough for me. I got eyes...' He turned and shot a quick

128

look at Brandon. 'Whoa,' he said, 'I just got that. You mean we didn't protect the fence?'

Brandon looked significantly at the breaks in the wire. 'They came through, didn't they?' he said, then he rubbed a hand over his face. 'No – I didn't mean that. Tired, I guess.'

An awkward silence fell over the group. The sun bore down upon them. No one spoke until the wagon came creaking up. Cal was on the seat with Emory, the dark man, his pale eyes were squinted up tighter than ever when he saw the trampled feed and the shattered fence. He sighed, and swore, running his eyes up and down it, shook his head mournfully and climbed down.

'Lot of work to do now.'

Brandon looped his reins through the rear wheel of the wagon. 'Let's get started.'

One of the riders got up off the ground and said: 'I could eat a skunk if someone'd hold its head.'

Brandon was pulling his gloves on. 'We'll eat twice as much when we get the fence fixed. I told you fellers this wouldn't be any picnic when I hired you. Let's get going.'

They worked, all six of them, Cal doing what he could, which wasn't much, and the four riders working gingerly and awkwardly, warily at first, then they got the hang of the job and made rapid strides toward completing the distasteful undertaking. Brandon finally gave Cal the reins of his black horse and had him ride up on a nearby knoll. When the others were finished with the fence, Cal rode back down toward them with a wry expression.

'Didn't see a soul. Just critters.'

They drifted back to the ranch with the sun hurling its heat-weight across the shoulders and down one side. Sweat stood out on the animals and the men were silent. Inside Brandon was a cold fury as big as the faded, brassy sky overhead.

Chapter Five

Brandon was over in the blacksmith's shop shoeing his grulla horse when Cal came over, stepped into the dingy shade and jerked his head sideways.

'Rider coming.'

Brandon straightened up, flipped sweat off his forehead and laid aside the tongs. 'Just one. Who is it?'

'I don't know. Them hired men of yours slipped around behind the bunkhouse just in case.'

Brandon reached for his shirt, struggled into it and went outside bareheaded. In the wavy distance he could see a horseman. One glance was enough. He went back, got his hat and walked across the yard, shoving his shirt-tail inside his breeches. 'Tell the boys to come out in the open, Cal. I know who it is. A friend.'

By the time Charley Belton rode into the yard the four riders were lounging in the shade of the bunkhouse, owl-eyed, unmoving. He cast a long glance at them and reined over near the house, where Brandon was standing. Neither man spoke right away. Charley reined up and swung down with a nod.

'Howdy, Brandy. How's the fence war coming?'

'It isn't. I've been set down on twice now.'

Charley walked up into the meager shade in the front of the house. 'Hotter'n a lizard's insides.' He jerked a thumb toward Cal, who was with the other men over by the bunkhouse. 'What happened to him, rope burns?'

Brandon shook his head. 'Someone tied him up with barbed wire.'

Charley looked startled. 'On the wrists? I'll be damned.'

'How're things in town?'

'Not so good.' Charley gazed up at the front of the old house. 'The sheriff was over yesterday. Damned near was another war. Town Fathers're up in arms over him letting you go. He got pretty hot over them saying they wouldn't have Sam Morton or Ed Spanner for Town Marshal and local deputy. I thought for a while there was going to be a fight.'

'Who got the job then?'

Charley fished deep in his trouser pocket, pulled out his fist and opened it. 'Me,' he said. Brandy recognized the badge. Their eyes met over it. 'I'll tell you, Brandy. It was me or an outsider. The sheriff – you know he's a kind of a pin-headed cuss – swore he'd bring in some saddlebum from Fallbrook. The town paws said they'd throw his man in the lockup if he showed up over here wearin' a badge. Well,' Charley's shoulders rose and fell. 'By God, I hated to do it, but it was me or more trouble, so I took it.'

'I'm glad you did,' Brandon said. 'Now – you ought to have an idea who's behind this fence cutting.' He told Charley about the cattle stampeded through the fence the night before.

Charley looked at the dusty ground in a thoughtful way. 'I can't even guess close, Brandy. I honestly can't. There's no talk around town.' He raised his eyes. 'You been sitting out there hoping to catch them?'

'Yeah. Every night.'

Charley shot a twisted look toward the bunkhouse. 'Those aren't the same fellers who were here last time I rode out, are they?'

'No, I hired them over in Fallbrook. I don't know yet how tough they are, but if looks count for anything they'll do.'

'Yeah,' Charley said slowly. 'Brandy, the town's split up. The range is split up. Can't we figure a way to settle this mess before all hell busts loose?'

'Sure. That's simple enough. Get the cowmen to lay off that fence. That's all it'll take.'

'Real simple,' Charley said dryly. 'In town the riders are betting you won't last another two weeks – you and the fence. I can't just see Jared and Fat Spanner dropping things now.'

'Are they behind it?'

'Who knows?' Charley said. 'There's got to be proof, don't there, before I can lock anyone up?'

'Sure, and I'll tell you how to get it, Charley.'

'Fire away,' Charley said, 'but first off let me tell you something. If we don't settle things, Brandy, this is going to be a damned hot country for a while. Remember that before you turn those wolves loose over there by the bunkhouse. One shot'll get you ten.'

Brandon stiffened inside. His expression toward Charley Belton, his old friend, didn't alter. He wore a hard, withdrawn look. 'Well – to get back to the proof, Charley, there were at least three riders with those cattle last night.'

'What's that prove if you didn't see them?'

'Just listen for a minute, will you? It proves that you, as the law, can go to the ranches and find out which outfit had men riding last night.' He saw Charley's mouth move and hurried on. 'Sure – those places that had men off the place will say they were in town. You check with Frosty, the other bar-keepers, for the truth of that. Check every cowboy's girl if you have to. The liverybarn. It's pretty simple, Charley.'

'Yeah. Sounds awfully simple. I wish you had this job back again. The Town Fathers want you to take it back, too. That's one reason why I'm out here today. Oh yes – I darned near forgot – the sawbones'll be out today, too. How's Milt?'

'Eating good and looking a little better. He doesn't remember anything, though. Told me he didn't even hear the shot that downed him.'

'You aren't surprised at that, are you?'

'No.'

'Named the baby yet?'

Brandon's eyes lifted to the farthest horizon and stayed there. He knew what Charley was leading up to. 'Haven't hardly had time to look at it since I've been here.'

'How's Marti?'

'Fine. Come on; we'll go in and get a cup of coffee.'

But Charley said, 'No. Not this trip. An-other time. Will you take the badge back?'

'I can't, Charley. You know that. Where I'm concerned it'd just be the town mar-shal's badge and for what's going on here I'd need both badges again. The sheriff's dead set against me and you know it.'

'You know what that is. Politics.'

'Knowing doesn't change anything, Charley.'

'No.'

A silence settled briefly between them. Over in the corral several horses were hugging the side of the barn for shade and stomping lazily at flies. The riders had drifted down by the smithy where Cal was showing them the plow he'd rigged up for the team. Beyond the corrals was the range, dry and brown looking. It was a peaceful scene. Charley sighed.

'Brandy; if I find out who the fence cutters are...'

'Yes?'

'How the hell can I, a rancher, throw them in jail?'

'It's easy,' Brandon said bluntly. 'Just march them in and...'

'You know better than that.'

A shadow passed over Brandon's face. After a moment's silence he nodded and said: 'I guess I do, Charley, but you took the badge, pardner.'

'You know why I did that, too. Because if I'd stood back and let the sheriff send in a gunhand from his Fallbrook stable there'd be more'n just a fence war. Listen: this is like sitting atop a powder keg with a short fuse under you. Either way all hell may break loose, your fence or the fight between the Town Fathers and the sheriff. It's got the whole cussed country stirred up. All folks talk about. In town it's the feud with the sheriff. On the range and in the cow camps and saloons it's your damned fence. If Marti only knew what she'd... Well, squaw-talk won't help, will it?'

'No. Complaining never helps anything.' Brandon stood a moment in thought. 'Charley – it looks like I'll have to catch them myself.'

Charley set about making a cigarette. He said nothing. Brandon watched him complete the smoke, light it and exhale.

'You're in a spot.'

'Hell,' Charley said, almost exasperatedly. 'I'm worse'n that; I'm plumb hog-tied. Look, Brandy – if I help you the cow out-fits'll break me. If I help them, which I don't feel much like doing, I'd be against you and Marti. And if that isn't enough – what about keeping the folks over in Fallbrook and Fort Parker from having a little war all their own? You think *you* got troubles!' Brandy straightened up with a grunt. 'You know my hands're tied I just took this tomfool job to keep 'em off your back – if I could – and keep peace in town for as long as I can – all the time hoping to hell someone'll come along and straighten things out. It's a mess.

'You know what would've happened if Sam Morton or Ed Spanner had got the badge, but I can't come right out and help you and you ought to know that, too, since I've got to sit back and leave the fence business in your lap and just try to keep 'em from snagging you off as you ride by, sort of and keep the lid on the powder-keg in town.'

Brandon thought of something else that Charley hadn't mentioned, too. If Belton showed up on Brandy's side the same power that had shorn him of his authority would also pluck Charley. What a hell of a mess.

'You're right, Charley. As usual, you're plumb right.'

Charley picked up his reins, tugged them through his fingers. 'Not as usual,' he said, avoiding Brandon's face. 'Well; I'll slope, Brandy – and listen – do me one favor. If you're in town with your boys don't start any fights. That's all it'd take, believe me.'

Brandon didn't answer. Charley swung back into the saddle, sat there looking down at Brandon, shifted a little. 'Come on in some morning, Brandy. I'll buy you a breakfast.'

'All right. S'long.'

'S'long.' Charley's gaze went almost furtively to the house. 'Tell Marti hello for me.'

'Yeah.'

He stood out in the sun until Charley was small in the distance, then he went over where Cal was. The men were eyeing him

137

blankly. He didn't look up at them, held his gaze to the plow. 'Got it all hooked up, Cal?'

'Yeah, rigged for the team.'

'Good. Let's see what kind of "grangers" we'd make.'

Cal was watching him unblinkingly, the pale eyes full of questions. Brandon ignored the look. As they walked toward the corral Brandon explained what he wanted done. The cowboys were slow and awkward about doing it, but after they'd made a few round with the plow their spirits revived in spite of the drenching heat. With much profanity, hilarity, and cat-calling, they plowed an eighty foot wide circle around the ranch buildings. The task became a sweaty source of amusement to them, for none had ever operated a team on a plow before. The huge circle was ragged looking. No one wondered why they were doing it, it was a common enough practice. In the tall-grass cow-country in the late summer. Fire-break.

Brandon was back in the blacksmith's shop finishing the shoeing job he'd begun and could hear the shouts and laughter in the distance. From the doorless opening he could see the rich earth uprooted, flung over, leaving a rope-like coil of moldy earth behind the moldboard. It was a soothing sight to him, because he'd never been able to shake the fear that lived in every rangeman during the hot months, that fire, accidental or man made, could sweep over the tinder-dry feed on the range within a matter of minutes and destroy every building.

'Hello.'

He looked up, bent over the right rear foot with the rasp tilted between downward strokes. Marti, her hair caught up behind her head with the little green ribbon, like she wore it when she was working, was standing near the old anvil, cool, fresh looking, smiling.

'You look hot and tired.'

'Hot,' he said, dropping the horse's leg, straightening up, 'but not tired. How're your patients?'

'The doctor drove in a few minutes ago. Milton's doing fine. He's always hungry. The baby has a heat-rash.' She paused, looking up at him. 'Brandy; wasn't that Charley Belton's horse I saw in front of the house a while ago?'

'Yes. He – couldn't stay very long. Said to give you his regards.'

'Did he have any news?'

'Yes. He's the new Town Marshal.'

'Oh.'

He saw that she was regarding him with uncertainty, reached down and picked up the rasp, turned it in his hand. 'You look like you think that's wrong. It isn't, Marti. I wanted Charley to take the job when I stepped out. He can do us more good as the marshal than

139

anyone else can.'

'Do you mean about Milt?' She was looking at him steadily.

He tossed the rasp aside. 'Not specifically – not right now, anyway. That'll come out in time, though, I think. I meant in other ways.' He didn't want to pursue the subject with her so he spoke again before she could ask the question that was forming on her lips. 'Will the doctor be able to help the baby's heat-rash?'

It was so palpably weak that he saw her expression change to a mocking, knowing look. The funny feeling swept over him again, seeing her like that, with that mocking look, beside the age-darkened old anvil, the sooted walls of the smithy.

'You're close-mouthed when you want to be, aren't you?'

'Sometimes it's best, Marti.'

'All right.' From behind her she held up a tall glass. 'Lemonade. I thought you'd want it.'

He walked over close to her with something solid in his throat. With more boldness than he knew was in him he said: 'Marti – are you always like this? Sort of thoughtful and–' he almost had the word, but it eluded him. 'And smiling?'

'Why, Brandy? Do you want to be sure before you say anything you might be sorry for later?'

Her answer came back too quick. It threw him into confusion. He withdrew into his shell again and she could see him doing it, slipping away from her, the way his color came up. She pushed the glass at him almost angrily.

'Here, you big horse; I hope you choke.'

He drank soberly, watching her over the rim. Her eyes flashed up at him, the sturdy pulse in her throat was drumming erratically.

'I have to go to town. Can I use the wagon and one of your hired men?'

He set the glass on the anvil and felt fresh perspiration pop out on him. 'You'd better take two of them,' he said, thinking that one of the toughs might prove a handful; two wouldn't.

'I don't need but one.'

'You'd better take two anyway,' he persisted.

She picked up the glass and shot him a warm look. 'All right, Boss.' She turned away.

'Marti?'

She came around so lightly she might have been expecting him to speak her name like that. Went back to the edge of the anvil and leaned a little toward him.

'Yes?'

'Uh – be careful, won't you?'

She held his eyes with her own and very slowly shook her head back and forth until the little golden pony-tail waved from side to side like a banner. 'No, I don't think I will. I think I'll do something reckless.'

'What?'

'Or – you could give me something to think about while I'm riding in, then I wouldn't want to be reckless.'

'Oh.'

He bent and kissed her. She ran her hands up his bare arms to his shoulders, pulled him down over the anvil a little, then pushed him away. Very solemnly she said: 'Brandy, you're sticky. You need a bath.'

He took one after she'd gone, one of the riders tooling the team from beside her on the high seat, another trailing along behind, ahorseback, then he threw himself upon his bunk and slept. Outside, the other riders and Cal were unharnessing the steaming team and making derogatory remarks about one another's plowing prowess.

He slept until the shadows were long and it was the creaking of the wagon returning that awakened him. He got up, went out back, sluiced off, fingered his face, shaved, combed his hair and went out through the bunkhouse and across the yard where Marti was supervising the unloading of the wagon. Until he saw distant movement and turned to look at it, he'd forgotten that the doctor had been there altogether. An eruption of sound from the corral brought him around. Cal and another rider were snubbing a green colt.

'Good evening,' he smiled at her. 'You look like you've been out in the sun.'

Her cheeks were as red as apples, the hair at the nape of her neck hung in damp ringlets. She thrust out her lower lip and blew upwards at a stray, limp strand of blonde hair.

'I have been. Brandy, one of the cowboys who used to work here on the ranch is working in the liverybarn in town. You should have seen his embarrassment when he saw me. He looked like he wanted to drop through the floor.'

'Is that so? Did you see Charley?'

She looked at him oddly. 'No. Should I have?'

'No. Just thought you might is all.' An idea struck him. 'Are you sure about the cowboy at the liverybarn?'

'Of course I'm sure. I paid them off, didn't I?'

'What was his name?'

'Michael Fanning. He was the youngest one. Clean-shaven.'

'I remember him,' Brandon said. 'Marti? Don't tell Cal or the others you saw him.'

'All right,' she said, puzzled and showing it. 'Did *he* shoot Milton?'

'I doubt it. Our secret?'

'Yes. What's–?'

'How're things in town?'

She didn't answer right away. 'Someday,'

143

she said finally, flatly, 'you're going to do that to me and I'm not going to be meek and sweet, Mister Parker!'

'Do what?'

'Do what?' She mimicked him with a smoky look. 'Switch the subject like I'm a child and you're leading me away from something you don't want to talk about – that's what.'

He watched her. 'Marti; there's a word that fits you. I've tried a hundred times to think of it. It's a funny little word.' He stopped speaking for a moment. They were close. 'You're as cute as a tick's ear when you look like that; sort of mad.'

She sniffed. 'It's still changing the subject,' she said, but her voice had lost its snap. 'And I'm not really mad.' She looked up toward the house. 'I've got to run.'

He watched the men unloading the wagon for a moment longer then went over to the bunkhouse. One of his hired men was changing a torn shirt. He threw a hard grin at Brandon.

'Damned colt piled me.'

Brandon sat down wordlessly at the table and smoothed out a scrap of paper. 'I want you to take this note to the Town Marshal at Fort Parker. Make as good time as you can and don't talk to anyone but the Marshal. Understand?'

'Yeh.'

When Brandon folded the paper and handed it to the rider he said: 'You can make it back to the ranch a little after suppertime if you make tracks. We'll be looking for you.'

He went with the man, to the barn, helped him saddle a horse and when the rider loped away he waved carelessly at the other men who were looking after him. Brandon then went idly over by the corral, watching Cal and another man manhandling a green colt.

When Marti rang her cow bell for supper, Cal climbed out of the corral and fell in beside Brandon. 'We goin' out again tonight?'

Brandon looked at the lowering sun and wondered if his messenger would find Charley in town. 'I don't know, Cal,' he said finally. 'Haven't made up my mind yet.'

Marti had the table set. In a back room the baby was snuffling his distress at the heat. Marti shot him a harassed look. The high flush was still in her face. She motioned for the men to be seated then went down the hall with a tray for Milton.

Brandon, Cal, the three Fallbrook riders, ate alone. Brandon kept waiting for Marti to come back, but she never did. Not until the meal was over and the men had gone outside for their after-supper smoke. He was moving toward the door when she appeared and called him softly.

'Brandy.'

He turned back, letting the door swing

closed. 'Yes'm?'

'Milton wants to see you.'

He followed her to the boy's bedroom. Milt was sitting up. His face was sharply thin, but the color was good. There was a little of the old sparkling sheen to his eyes.

'Want to see me, Milt?'

'Yeah. I've been thinking back, Marshal.'

'My name's Brandon, and I'm not the Marshal any more.'

Milton ducked his head. 'All right,' he said. 'Brandon then. I do remember something, only it probably doesn't have anything to do with the shooting. Someone was riding behind me. I heard them a couple of times. The last time was a few minutes before I got shot.'

'Which side of the fence, Milt?' Brandon asked, perplexed. A rider *behind* Milton would have had to have been on the ranch, inside the fence.

'On our side. That's why I didn't pay much attention. Didn't think it worth mentioning until now. I figured at the time it must be a loose horse, or something like that.'

Brandon stood gazing at Milt lost in thought. The boy had been shot from across the fence; he knew that for a fact. If it had been a horseman behind him, then he would have had to have been following Milt from the ranch, probably, and if so – why? So *he* could ambush the kid? It was a puzzler. He

146

nodded unconsciously. 'How're you feeling?'

'Oh, a lot better. The doc was by today. He said I'd be up and around in another couple of weeks. Say, Marsh – Brandon, would you teach me how to draw a gun when I'm up?'

'You mean draw a gun fast?'

'Yeah.'

'Well; seems to me you've got other things to learn first, Milt.'

'What? Like what?'

'How to hold your tongue and act your age,' Brandon said bluntly.

Milton's eyes widened. His mouth began to get that set look to it.

Brandon raised his eyebrows and shrugged. 'Milt; there're a hundred men in the Fort Parker country that would have killed you for talking to them like you talked to Charley Belton, and every last one of them could do it blindfolded and left-handed. You've got to understand that before I'll even stand by and watch you wear a gun, let alone teach you how to use it.'

Milton's eyes were like wet iron, but he didn't say a word. Marti brushed Brandon's sleeve. Coolly she said: 'Come on, Brandy, he needs rest.'

Brandon went around the bed, lingered a moment. 'Milt, I roughed up your hide and I know it, but, there just isn't any other way to tell you about this country than straight out. Thanks for telling me about the horse.'

Milton didn't look at Brandon as he and Marti left the room. His face was stormy looking; had that peculiar leashed-violence look to it Brandon and Charley Belton had noticed the first day they'd ridden up.

Back in the kitchen Marti turned on him. 'Why did you have to upset him, Brandy? He's only a boy. I thought you'd have–'

'Marti, when a feller packs a gun and is itching to use it it's usually because he's a boy. Milt wouldn't stand the chance of a pig in a wolf's den with two-thirds of the men in this country, and whether you're being threatened by a gun in the hands of a kid or a killer, the bullet is just as big. I wanted to get my licks in before he got up and started swaggering around again. It's for his own good and yours. I think he'll sort of mull it over: it's a cinch he can't go anywhere, so he'll have to do a little thinking. Maybe by the time he's up, he'll be wiser.'

'But you sounded so – so – tough.'

Brandon smiled at her. 'I'm not tough. Never was. Listen, Marti; if it wasn't for you I wouldn't horn in with Milt, but I don't want to see you hurt.' He crossed to the peg on the wall, took his hat down and turned back to face her. 'I'm going to take the boys over to the fence tonight. Maybe the raw-hiders'll be back.'

'Rawhiders?'

'Folks who make trouble. Troublemakers

– rawhiders, sort of an expression we use in the Fort Parker country.'

She ran her hand over the upswept side of her hair. 'Aren't we rawhiders, too, Brandy? We're making trouble with the fence. Can't we let it go?'

He stiffened perceptibly. 'It's your fence. You can call me off any time you want to, ma'm.'

Seeing his expression she said: 'No, of course I wouldn't do that – exactly – only – the trouble, and all. The fear every time...' She crossed the room and stood in front of him. 'We'll be rawhiders if you catch fence cutters, Brandy.'

He inclined his head once. 'I hope we get the chance, ma'm,' he said. 'One of these nights they won't outsmart us. All I ask is one good lick at them. Just one.'

She forced a smile. 'See you in the morning, Brandy.'

He was so absorbed with his thoughts he forgot to kiss her. Just smiled vacantly and went out of the house.

Darkness wasn't far off. He sniffed at the night, at the cow-country smell, the writhing, leaching heat that arose all around him bearing scents upwards from the grass, earth, the brush patches.

'Hey, Brandon! How about us goin' to town tonight?'

He went toward the familiar figure. 'I've

149

changed my mind, Cal. I think we'd better ride the fence tonight.' He watched the flared nostrils, the dead-alive eyes. There wasn't a flicker of expression, not even disappointment. Cal turned toward the bunkhouse without a word and Brandon followed him.

'Saddle up, boys, we're goin' fence ridin' again.' Cal said it without any especial inflection. Behind him in the doorway, Brandon watched. The three riders threw down their cards and stood up. One, with scrupulous honesty, divided the poker-pot three ways. The men pocketed their money, went to their bunks, grabbed booted carbines and headed out the bunkhouse door.

Brandon trailed them to the corrals to get horses and into the barn to saddle up. They mounted in silence and rode through the gloom exactly as they'd done before. The dark man, Emory, edged in beside Brandon and asked if they were going to do as they'd done the night before. Brandon said, 'Yes,' and that was all he said until they were close to the fence.

By then it was dark with a thick scudding of ghostly clouds overhead and a foreign, metallic-tasting dankness in the atmosphere. Brandon threw his head back and looked upward. A ground-washing breeze rustled low in the grass. It smelt of rain. Far off along the lifting line of the horizon there was a brief flicker of lightning. Brandon watched, then gazed upward again where the stars shone mistily, half alight, moist looking. His nostrils quivered. The first storm of early Fall was in the air. He stood in his stirrups, heard the creak of other saddles around him and sniffed at the air, the night, the dark ground. Rain would come, if not tonight then tomorrow. The range was acid-etched against the lighter, less solid look of the night and when the lightning came there was no thunder with it. A peculiar feeling of urgency stirred deep within him. He studied the land as far as he could see. It was as dark as it would be all night, until dawn, and the three-quarters moon cast an opalescence that was flat and glowing. When the huge rolls of clouds passed before it their edges turned a soft, dirty silver color. He moved in his saddle, felt the smoothness of the leather, squinted when the moon was obscured, the land plunged into abysmal darkness that lasted five minutes. Another glance upward showed him that this would happen all night long, until the clouds either merged or dissipated. Light one moment, darkness the next. Damn the cowmen, damn the moonlight. He turned in the saddle.

'You,' he said, pointing to one of the men, 'you go due west but stay out of sight of anyone across the fence. If they've got men watching we don't want to be seen. Stay well back, find a knoll and crawl up to it. Don't skyline your horse. Use the match flare if you see anything or hear anything. Understand?'

The man nodded and reined away. Brandon thumbed toward another man. 'You stay about where we are now. Keep out of sight of the fence and use the match flare too.'

He turned to Cal and Emory. 'You two come with me.' He led them east on a northerly, angling course that kept them all well away from the fence. None of them spoke as they rode. A cloud fled across the face of the moon and with one movement all three men looked up at it.

Emory said: 'We could use some rain.'

Brandon watched the folds of the range open out around him as the cloud went by overhead, the light came gushing in pale splendor again. Some small dark squares northward, well inside the fence, were Grant ranch cattle. As they rode by, the animals stood up, joints creaking, heads high, motionless. There was electricity in the air; their eyes shone wetly, restlessly. Southward there was nothing. There could have been a big herd of cattle or an army, Brandon couldn't see far.

He rode all the way to the stage road and out through the Grant ranch gate. Cal made a cigarette and exchanged a significant look with Emory, and Brandon waited until he had the match under his thumb then said

'Don't!' Cal held the match without striking it. He shrugged and put it into his shirt pocket. The unlit cigarette dangled.

Brandon cut south, down across the free-range. He rode a little ahead of the other two, made for every knoll and rode far enough up each one to see over the top and down the other side without being seen himself. They rode like that for an hour, time seeming to merge with monotony before Brandon stopped, sat still listening. Except for the barely heard, haunted, low moan of the breathing earth, there wasn't a sound. Just that bony little breath of wind along the ground. The metallic taste of forthcoming rain. Brandon's thoughts were glass-clear, uncomplicated. The rawhiders always come from the south; Grant ranch riders had always waited for them. Offense, defense; well, he'd change that. Grant ranch would usurp the offense. *They'd* be outside the fence this time. His mouth curled – then the cowmen wouldn't come, probably.

He lifted his reins when the next moment of stygian darkness came. Rode westerly, paralleling the fenceline but deep within the out-range and the stillness became oppressive. Even the little scurrying breeze had died. When he stopped for the second time the other two men swung up on either side of him. The moonwash glowed on their metal accouterments, on the ivory butt of Emory's

153

gun. Neither rider seemed disposed to talk, their eyes were soft, wet, in the paleness. Emory's horse ducked his head and snorted softly. Emory's lips moved in a curse, but softly. The night had its grip on each one of them. The animal's head came up.

Cal said, 'We can't see no flares from here.'

Brandon lifted his reins and rode on again without answering. He had a feeling... Wanted to listen to the night every chance he got. He angled north a little, toward the fence. Inwardly he knew with grim satisfaction that if the cowmen came again, were around him somewhere now, they would more than likely assume he was north of the fence, not carrying war beyond it into their own domain. He hoped they would think like that. He might not find them or they might not show up, but at least they wouldn't make a fool out of him the third time.

He twisted a little in his saddle toward Emory. 'See that landswell yonder on your right? Ride over there, leave your horse at the bottom of it. Crawl up. You'll be able to see a lot of fence. Take a good look, then catch up with us, we'll be going west.'

Emory turned his horse toward the knoll. Cal moved closer as he and Brandon rode on. 'I don't think they'll be out here tonight.'

'Why don't you?'

Cal gestured at the dark-shadowed range. 'Poor night to see. Anyway, seems to me they come earlier'n this, mostly.'

Irritably Brandon said, 'They don't run on a schedule any more'n we do.'

'No – it's just a feeling I got.'

Brandon said no more. He twisted in his saddle. Couldn't see Emory coming after them or hear him either. The irritation grew. As he was turning again movement snagged at the edge of his vision. He reined up sharply and looked. A horseman was coming straight toward them in a fast walk. He said, 'Wait,' and Cal also stopped.

When the rider got close the moon burst from behind a cloud. It was Emory and he was making an excited motion at them with his right arm. Brandon rode back toward him.

'See anything?'

'Yeah – but not up there.' He pointed westward. 'Down there – a match.'

Brandon's nerves tingled. 'They came from down country this time, then. Good. Let's go.'

They rode at a walk, fearing to lift their animals into a faster gait, the sound of three galloping horses would carry a mile in the milky silence. It was an agonizingly long ride. What didn't take twenty minutes seemed like half the night. When they were about parallel with the second man Brandon had stationed inside the fence, they were a good mile south of the fence.

Brandon swung his horse northward in a straight line toward the fence and made an outflung motion with his arm in indicating Emory should ride farther out, away from him and Cal. They went a hundred yards, two hundred yards. Brandon signaled for Emory to stop, then he swung down and handed his reins to Cal and began to climb a sloping hillock dead ahead.

From the top, prone, he could see the fence gleaming in the middle distance. He lay perfectly still, listening, looking for the flare of a match that never came. Westward, down the fence, a cloud-shadow hung over the portion of the fence he looked at. It obscured the fence and the range on both sides of it for a quarter of a mile. He swore to himself, waiting for the shadow to drift away.

When it finally left he saw nothing, had his hands under him to press upward with when a horse blew his nose off to Brandon's left somewhere. He froze. Another horse did the same thing and his heart thudded against his ribs. Two horses, at least, out there somewhere. He had only left one man across the fence. One man, one horse. He crawled off the eminence, got to his feet and trotted back to Cal, took his reins and yanked the grulla horse under him, threw up his arm and waved Emory in.

'There are at least two horses west of us.'

'Shouldn't be but one,' the dark man said.

156

'You see 'em?'

'No, just heard 'em. There's some brush down there and a damned shadow blocked off my view for a while, but anyway, there's only supposed to be one man there. Let's keep together and go down a ways.'

They rode quietly for another ten minutes, found another landswell, not as high as the first, and Brandon gestured for Emory to go up and held out his hands for the dark man's reins. Cal was tense. Brandon understood that because he was tense himself. Emory came trotting back with a wide smile. The moon shone feather-soft off him, made his teeth look like ice.

'We got company all right. Four of 'em that I could see. They're working up toward us cutting the fence.'

'Where are their horses?'

'Damned if I know. Tied down the fence somewhere I expect.'

Brandon handed over Emory's reins and looked around at Cal. 'Well, how would you work it?' he asked.

'Easy,' Cal said. 'I'd find their horses and stampede them. That's how we used to do with Indians years back. Set 'em afoot and you got 'em.'

Brandon nodded, studied the greasy, be-whiskered face with its pale eyes a moment, then said: 'That's it, I reckon.'

Emory had his rein hand poised, his teeth

showing in a wolfish smile. 'Let's go. I been waitin' for this,' he said.

Brandon turned his horse and rode in a big circle so as to get below the fence cutters. He could feel the hair at the base of his skull standing straight up. And yet a thin flowing warmth of triumph was running in his veins, too. This was his night: Grant ranch's night.

'There,' Cal said suddenly. 'Yonder at the fence.'

The dark man pulled his horse up short; the animal made a startled sound. A shiver ran down Brandon's back. There were horses over near a clump of brush, but there were also two men that Brandon could see. He swung around, backtracked, with Cal and Emory following his example. When they were hidden from the sight of the men standing with the horses, Brandon stepped down and held his reins out to Cal with a searching look at the older man's face.

'Here I'll take another loo–'

Someone whistled, a high, trilling sound of warning.

Emory let off a curse and the sound of his carbine sliding out of its boots made a dry, slithering sound. The moonwash caught the barrel, limned it. Brandon swung back toward his horse.

The whistle came again, higher, more in-sistent.

'Something's wrong,' Cal said, holding Brandon's reins out to him. 'They heard us or seen us.'

Brandon had his toe in the stirrup when the earth shook under them. The rumble of running horses shattered the stillness.

'There!' Emory yelled, fighting to bring his carbine around. 'There – comin' aroun' that goddamn knoll.' He fired. A lancet of pale flame snaked dagger-like into the gloom. Brandon's horse shied. He fought its head.

Three riders broke into view as they cleared the sloping edge of the knoll. Two more were spurring behind them. Something like a hundred feet separated the first men from the last. With the echo of Emory's shot still vibrating in the heavy air two pistols shredded the darkness in answer.

Brandon clawed for his hand-gun, got it out. Cal fired once, then again, using his six-gun. The dirty white of his bandaged wrist jerked each time he fired. Brandon brought his own gun up at the exact moment the two trailing fence cutters threw down. Gunshots bracketed the area, made it flicker with orange light and deafening sound. Somewhere, far behind the fleeing men, someone shouted and fired. One of the rearmost riders went down, his horse hit. The animal lay asprawl, never moved. The rider leapt up. He had a carbine in one fist. Emory flung off his horse, knelt and aimed. The upset fence cutter threw himself behind his dead horse. Emory fired and in spite of the weak light they could all see the dead horse's carcass jerk with impact. The embattled man fired back. Cal Stephans slumped lower, lower, and fell...

Brandon swung his horse ahead, kicked him out and slammed two rapid shots at the partially protected fence cutter. The man half leapt upright, fell across his horse.

The rider Brandon had left across the fence came up in a dust-spewing slide. His carbine, cocked, rode lightly in one fist, his mouth was open as though to shout, but no noise came. Brandon recognized him and turned back, dismounted and went over to where Emory was kneeling beside Cal. In the damp night, with silence drenching them again, Emory twisted his head upward, toward Brandon.

'Right through the lights.'

'We've got to get him to the ranch.'

Emory eased Cal's gray face down and stood up. 'I'll go fetch the wagon and a mattress.'

'Yeah,' Brandon said, without looking round. 'Make time.'

The remaining rider stepped off his horse, craned his neck then turned and looked over where the dead fence cutter lay. 'I got his horse from behind.' He turned toward Brandon. 'What in hell kept you fellers?

Chris', I used up most all my matches makin' flares.'

Brandon's face was chalky. He dropped to one knee beside Cal. His answer came over one shoulder. 'We saw your flare once – Emory did. That's probably what they saw, too, because one of 'em whistled a warning – they ran for it then.'

'Well,' the rider said, staring hard at Cal's still face. 'Well...'

'Go get that dead one's carbine, will you?' When the rider walked away, the sound of his spurs faint, musical, Brandon leaned closer. 'Cal? Can you hear me, Cal?'

The pale, dead-alive eyes opened, looked up. A froth of black looking blood formed thick on Cal's lips. 'They've gone?'

'One isn't,' Brandon said. 'The one that shot you isn't.' Cal, closed his eyes, his lips moved, slowly, closed loosely and hung that way. Brandon felt helpless. There wasn't anything he could do. He stood up. The rider came back with two carbines, handed one to Brandon watched him lever it open, peer inside. The gun was empty. Brandon closed it, raised it overhead, fired it, levered out the empty casing, caught it and held it up to catch the faint moonlight. The pin hit high, off-center. Under the uncomprehending stare of his cowboy, he dropped the casing into his shirt pocket, lowered the gun and stood there, his back to the dead fence cutter, the deep well of the night around him, earthy-damp smelling, as still and silent as a tomb.

Chapter Six

The noise of the wagon going out and coming back awakened Marti. She had a lamp burning in the house. Brandon saw it from half a mile away as they brought Cal in. There was another light in the bunkhouse, a man's silhouette in front of it outlined against the warming night, erect, motionless.

He dismounted and handed his reins to someone. The man he had sent to town with the note for Charley came off the bunkhouse stoop, lifted one side of the old mattress, and they bore Cal inside. Brandon went back to see if someone had taken care of the horses and met Marti coming across the yard.

'Brandy – help me with these.'

He took the pan with hot water in it, several yards of bleached muslin bandaging, and noticed that the moonlight made her golden hair look silver. It aged her, made her aloof, distant looking. Her eyes were almost black, her mouth drawn inward. She looked into his face and swung away, moved briskly toward the bunkhouse. He followed.

The room was crowded and smelt of men, horsesweat, gun oil and coal oil from the lamp, which smoked fitfully because no one ever bothered to trim the wick of a bunk-house lamp. The heat was stifling inside. Brandon jerked his head at the Fallbrook men, they followed him outside. One stumbled over the carbine Brandon had brought back with him, cursed it and kicked it aside, into the dust of the yard, off the stoop.

'Catch us all fresh horses, boys. We're going to ride into town.'

Emory's head bobbed up and down. 'Damn' right,' he said. They all went to-gether, four bulky silhouettes moving sound-lessly except for the ripple of spur-rowels. Brandon went back inside. Marti had Cal naked to the waist. Her face was pinched-white, bleak looking, a strand of hair lay in a curve across her forehead. The basin with the water was blood-red and trailings of steam arose from it. Cal looked dead.

Brandon shuffled his feet, moving closer. 'I'm goin' into town with the boys, Marti.'

No answer. The profile didn't turn. The hands were like frantic birds, here, there, moving, working.

'Want to see Charley Belton. We killed one of them. The one that shot Cal. Charley'll have to know.'

163

'Is there any chance the others might come here?' she said, still without looking up at him.

'No. I hardly think so, but I'll leave a man here if you'd rather.' He considered it. It wasn't likely, still– 'All right; I'll leave two of them here.'

'Send the doctor back, Brandy.'

'Yes'm. Well…'

'Go on.'

He went out to the waiting men, picked out two and left them behind. One cowboy besides Emory rode with him. They pushed their horses through the lowering night. The moon was hidden altogether, the clouds had merged to form a gray, gloomy blanket, there was a close heat to the air, the stars were murky looking, those he could see.

Like phantoms they went over the dark night-scape huddled close, the creak of metal, of leather, the only sound left in their wake, and when Fort Parker loomed up a soft, almost unheeded drizzle began. It wasn't like most first rains of Fall. They usually came with the crackle of close lightning, the accompaniment of kettledrum thunder, the big, hurtling wall of water. This was different. The rain began very gently, drizzled, warm, soothing. Their clothes got darker, their hats and saddles and horses, and their metal parts shone dully. Everything but their faces grew darker from the water.

Brandon was in a lope when he swung into town from the northern approach, the drizzle muting the sound of his horse's hooves making hollow, moist sounds. He rode the full length of town in a lope, echoes running ahead of him, bouncing off darkened saloons, stores, houses, the jangle of his equipment sounding extra loud, and right behind him Emory and the Fallbrook cowboy. There were a few lights, but only a few. One was at the Marshal's office. Brandon reined up and stepped down, flung his head sideways to throw off the accumulation of rain that dripped off his hat, and waited for his companions to dismount.

They pushed through the door, all three of them hard-eyed, worn and disheveled looking. To Brandon's eyes everything looked the same except that Charley Belton, not Brandon Parker, was behind the desk. Charley looked up, then got up. His gaze flicked from one face to another. He said nothing, didn't move.

Brandon took off his hat and slapped it against his leg. Spoke without looking up. 'Did you get my note, Charley?'

'Yeah, I got it.'

'Pick him up?'

'He's in the cell. Is that why you came in, Brandy?' Obviously Charley didn't think it was – not at three o'clock in the morning.

'Not altogether,' Brandon said. 'Can I talk

to him?'

'Sure. Just a second.' Charley went out around his desk toward the cell-room door.

Brandon let off a rattling sigh, tossed his wet hat aside, crossed to the stove, poked its ashes, fed in some kindling, got a spindling fire going and stood with his back to it. 'You fellers might just as well sit down,' he said to his riders. 'Or dry out by the stove. We'll get some coffee when we're through here.'

Emory's black eyes were rimmed with shiny pouches of flesh. He looked tired. 'You going to tell him about the one we killed?'

'In time,' Brandon said absently, watching the cell-room door swing inward.

Charley Belton poked the youth with him farther into the room. 'That's him, Brandy. His name's Fanning.'

'I know,' Brandon said. 'Michael Fanning. Sit down, Fanning.'

The youth looked chalky in the guttering light of an overhead lamp. His eyes, dry, swift-moving, kept coming back to the tall, unsmiling, bedraggled man over by the stove.

'Fanning; why did you trail Milt the night he got shot?'

'I never did no such thing,' the youth said. 'I went back to the bunkhouse after the poker game.'

Brandon nodded agreeably. 'All right,' he said. 'I can't prove you didn't, so I reckon you did.' He knew Charley was looking at him in a surprised way, disapprovingly. 'Tell me why you quit the Grant ranch, will you?'

'Sure. They was headin' for trouble with the big outfits. I ride for a living not fight. Besides, I didn't hardly think that fence was right, myself.' Fanning's voice was gathering strength as he talked. He moved his hands in his lap. Brandon looked at them, back up to his face.

'That's your right, too, isn't it?' He raised his gaze a little, looked at Charley. 'You can lock him up now, Charley. That's all I wanted.'

Fanning stood up. 'You got no right to keep me in here without saying what I done.'

Charley was frowning, first at the youthful rider, then at Brandon. He apparently felt pretty much the same way.

'Go ahead, Charley, put him back.'

'I've got to charge him, Brandy. You know that.'

Brandon shook his head. 'Protective custody'll hold him until daylight. After that I'll give you a charge.'

Charley opened the door, jerked his head at Fanning. The cowboy started to say something. Charley reached out, closed a big fist over his shoulder and tugged. Echoes of Fanning's voice haunted the office until Charley came back, slammed the door, shot Brandy a look and sank down behind his desk.

'Look, Brandy – what in hell's on your mind?'

Brandon walked over to the desk, fished out the spent cartridge casing from his shirt pocket and dropped it on the desk. 'That,' he said.

'I've seen this before,' Charley said, gazing closely at the casing. 'What about it?'

Brandon dredged its mate from his trouser pocket and dropped it on the desk, too. Charley's chair squeaked. He leaned forward, the annoyance wiped from his features. He picked up both casings and looked at them. The rain was increasing outside. It drummed with steady insistence on the roof. A tumbling gust of wind broke over the building, carrying the rain in whip-like streamers in its wake. The storm's momentum was gathering force.

'Same gun, Brandy.'

The voice sounded deep, solid, in the room. Emory crossed in front of the stove and stood there, hands clasped behind him, watching and listening.

'Yeah, it was the same gun. That's one thing I came in to tell you. The other thing's that the man who owned that gun shot Cal, that pale-eyed feller who rode for Marti, and I shot – killed – him.' He turned with a weary shake of his head. 'Emory; go get the doctor out of bed and started for the ranch, will you?'

'Sure.'

Charley put the casings down carefully. 'Did you recognize him?'

Brandon nodded. 'Yes. I knew who he was when I saw him bust out from behind a knoll. Recognized him from being on a few roundups with him in years past, and from seeing him ride around town, here. Sam Morton, Wagonwheel's foreman.'

Charley let his breath out slowly, picked up the casings again, peered at them a moment, then opened a desk drawer and dropped them in it, closed the drawer and automatically felt for his tobacco sack. 'Sam Morton. You killed him, Brandy?'

'Yes.'

The rain thundered against the roof like a million tiny fists.

'Your cowboy dead?'

'He wasn't when we left the ranch. Shot through the lungs though. Marti's taking care of him.'

Charley got up, went over by the stove, leaned, touched his cigarette to the stovepipe, inhaled a wisp of smoke, straightened up and faced around. His lips, around the cigarette, were thin and flat. 'Well,' he said, 'we know who potted Milt, then, don't we?' Brandon was easing himself down into the slat-bottomed chair. He didn't reply. 'We know who plugged Milt and we know who one of the riders was who was cutting her

169

fence. Where's that put us?'

'They brought it to us, Charley. They've been cutting that fence as regular as we fixed it. They stampeded stock through it and shot one of our boys who was trying to protect it.'

'True,' Charley said, his eyes distant looking. 'It's all true, but how about the rest of it; the town, the fight shaping up between the sheriff and the Town Fathers? It's all tied in together, Brandy. Killing Morton's going to blow the lid off it.'

'It was a justified killing. Self-defense. The law says–'

'I know I read it. Anyway, it isn't just Morton. Lord knows he was no great loss. I'm thinking about all of it. What'll happen now?'

Brandon's glance dropped to the stove a moment. 'I expect we all know the answer to that one, Charley. Damned range war.'

Charley straightened, a little gust of smoke spurted upward from his mouth. 'That's exactly what I've been trying to head off,' he said, then, in an angrier tone: 'That god-damned fence!'

Brandon stood up. The pounding rain made the room sound hollow. 'You'd better send out to pick Morton up, Charley, and send word to Wagonwheel – officially, I mean – because they'll know what happened to him by now. I'm going back. If you want me I'll be on the ranch.'

Charley nodded. Brandon went outside.

The rain was pelting down in sheets, slanting under the steady wind pressure. Emory came hugging up the plankwalk under the overhang. He swore when they were standing there together.

'I'd trade my saddle for my poncho right now or my slicker.'

'Get the doctor headed out?'

'Yeah, but he sure wasn't pleasant about it.'

Brandon looked down at something he'd taken from Charley's desk. A dull, silvery-looking deputy sheriff's badge that reflected the steely rain in his palm. He closed his fist around it, dropped the badge into his pants pocket and hunched up his shoulders. 'Let's go.'

They slopped down into wet-shiny saddles and Emory swore again. He was all bunched up like a frosted owl. Their horses' feet sounded sloppy as they walked northward, back toward the upper end of town and the faintest reflection of moonlight or starlight lay in the pools of rainwater they passed. At the end of town Brandon reined up, his face slippery looking, pinched up around the eyes.

'You fellers head back. I'll be along directly. I want to see a man first. Stoke up the fire in the bunkhouse.'

He didn't wait for their surprised looks, but reined right and went slogging at a walk around the end of some buildings and down a dismal alleyway where debris lay in wet, random piles. When he came to the blacksmith's shop he swung down, heard the squish of his boots against the soggy earth, tossed his limp reins around an ornamental lion's head hitching post and stomped to the doorway of a house set back behind the smithy.

It took a lot of pounding to arouse anyone and when the man who opened the door peered out over his spectacles, it was with a mean, unwelcome look in his eyes.

'It's me, Brandon.'

'Oh.'

The face faded from behind the lantern in the man's hand. 'Come in out o' the rain, Brandy. What a tarnation night!' The lantern bobbed sideways. 'Stand over there. Yeah, on that dog-mat. The old lady gets madder'n a stuck hog if you traipse water all over her house. Now then – I'm sure glad you came by. I suppose Charley's told you about that dumb-bell sheriff and his high ways. Well, I think we've got the kink yanked out of his tail.'

'That's partly why I'm here. The cowmen've been cutting the Grant ranch fence almost every night. Tonight we caught some of them doing it. There was a fight. A Grant ranch rider got shot through the chest and I killed Sam Morton.'

The spectacles, reflecting the lantern's

yellow glow, moved swiftly, jerkily. 'Sam Morton? Good God... You mean he was one of the cutters?'

'Him and four or five others.'

'What's Charley going to do – no, wait – we've got to get the Councilmen together, Brandy. Charley's too green to tackle this.' The blacksmith's labored breathing sounded particularly loud for a moment, because the wind sucked back the rain, left a second's silence, then the downpour returned.

'Sam Morton. Sam... Brandy; if Sam was one of them, Jared'll be another. Lord A'mighty! Probably Fat Spanner and the rest.' The smith leaned heavily on the door jamb: his nightshirt made him look huge and square. His eyes, behind the shiny glasses, looked large and owlish. 'What're you going to do now, boy?'

'Just wait; that's all we can do.'

'They'll come after you.'

'Maybe. I was on my way back to the ranch when I thought of you.'

'Sure glad you did.'

Brandon gripped the door latch with his fingers. 'I reckon Charley's going to need a hand through this,' he said.

'A hand,' the blacksmith said. 'Hell! He's going to need a fist, two of the – all he can get.'

Brandon lifted the latch, watching the blacksmith's face in the shadows. 'S'long.'

173

'Yeah, Brandy. S'long... Oh, hell!'

Brandon heard the last two words as he was closing the door. A shaft of rain-washed starlight flickered over his face, highlighting the faintest of humourless grins as he went toward his horse through the rain. He swung up and rode back out of town, reined west and a little south, boosting the animal into a sloppy gallop and holding him to it with his head bent low and the cold rain cutting through his clothes like flattened needles.

He wasn't sleepy, but his body was tired and by the time he made it back to the ranch the end of his spine was rubbed raw from contact with leather and soggy cloth. The buildings, when he eased down the last incline, looked like mottled squares of darkness with little squares of orange shining against them. The rain magnified the light, made it dance and shiver like Brandon was shivering when he unsaddled in the barn, forked the horse some hay, draped his saddle by the stirrup upon the wall, and shook water off his hat, then donned it again and trotted toward the bunkhouse.

Inside the warmth hit him like a wall. That, and the carbolic smell of the place. Marti wasn't there, but the riders were, and the doctor, wearing a funny little knitted hat, shot him a dark look from beneath his eyebrows and held up a freshly mixed bottle of something to the lamplight, gazed at the murky, dun-brown medicine, shook the bottle a little and put it on the bunkhouse table. Cigarette smoke was thick and murky. The iron stove was crackling and overhead the solitary lamp guttered every time a draught hit it.

'Get into some dry clothes,' the doctor said absently. 'Unless you want to catch your death.'

Brandy changed from the skin out, everything but his boots. He owned but one pair. While he re-dressed he beckoned Emory over. The dark man was bone-dry, and a cigarette hung from his slit of a mouth. Brandon was transferring his effects from wet pants to the ones he wore. When Emory was close he said, 'Listen,' in a low voice, 'I want you to ride over where we had that fight and stick this into the dead feller's pants pocket.' He opened his fist, dropped the deputy badge into Emory's palm and raised his eyes. The black gaze hung on his face for a moment, still, speculative, then Emory's lips pulled up a little. 'Sure,' he said. 'Right away.'

Brandon drew some attention away from Emory's leaving by walking over by the medical man. 'How's he look?'

'Look?' the doctor said, with no particular friendliness on his face. 'He looks more than half dead. What's going on out here, anyway?'

'The fence,' Brandon said. 'Remember?

When you came to here to patch Milton up you said–'

'I know what I said. Come over to the house with me, Brandy. Miss Grant said she'd make me some coffee and I need it – getting out of a warm bed, driving through a thunderstorm…'

Brandon covered his shoulders with his slicker. They squished side by side through the yard, which had become a millrace of streamlets, mud, and floating debris. On the veranda Brandon hung his slicker on a nail while the doctor rapped lightly. Marti swung the panel inward, her gaze jumping from the doctor's face to Brandon's. She had that pale, wax-like look he'd seen over Charley Belton's arm at the Fourth of July dance. They stomped their feet, scuffed them on an old feed sack, then went in. There was a bowl of doughnuts in the center of the table, two thick crockery cups, empty, waiting.

The doctor blew on his hands, scowling over them at the wall. Marti poured coffee silently. Brandon felt uncomfortable as he sat upright on his chair listening to the night, the rain and the bursts of wind that hurled themselves at the house fitfully, weaker.

'Will he live, Doctor?'

Brandon's eyes slowed to her face, her profile. There was a set look to her mouth, a smoky depth to her eyes. He squirmed inwardly. She hadn't said a word to him since they'd brought Cal back in the wagon. Then it had been short words, cold sounding.

The doctor bowed over his coffee, warming his hands around the cup. 'Well,' he said, 'I've seen a lot of them pull through shots in the lights. Of course, this weather may not help him any. If he gets cold it'll probably develop into pneumonia – then,' the doctor snapped his fingers, 'that'll be that.' He swung his head a little, toward Brandon. 'Is your fence worth all this? They tell me someone got killed out there tonight – last night.'

'Sam Morton got killed.'

'Sam… Treated him for a broken leg once. So Sam's dead…'

All the truthful things sounded futile to Brandon before he said them. Marti was stirring her coffee, looking at the oilcloth on the table. The doctor's repetition grated.

'Well – is it worth it?'

'We've got a fence,' Brandon said stolidly. 'We've made it stick so far.' He looked up at Marti who wasn't looking at either of them. 'I don't like this. Nothing'd suit me better'n to have them leave us alone.'

'Leave the fence alone, you mean,' the doctor said dryly.

'The fence too. We've made a play and we've got to back it up.'

The medical man's old eyes came up. 'Even if men get killed over it?'

'Yes, even then.'

The doctor drank his coffee, set the cup down and leaned far back in his chair. 'Then I reckon I'll just have to keep on making this trip every now and then until you all are either dead or too busted up to fight each other.'

'It isn't altogether us,' Brandon said, a little sharply. 'We're strictly within our rights.'

'I didn't mean just you, Brandy. I meant everyone who's involved. The fence cutters, too.'

Marti spoke for the first time. She looked levelly at Brandon. 'This man Morton, Cal, Milt, who'll be next, Brandy? I *told* you I didn't want to fight anybody.'

Brandon's ire rose up a little. His knuckles were white around the coffee cup. The doctor, looking down, noticed that. He cleared his throat. 'Let's talk it out a minute. Is there a way to stop the squabbling?' Marti said nothing. Brandon, looking at her, heard but didn't heed the words. The doctor looked from one to the other, then back at the tabletop again. He put his hands in his overcoat pockets and made as though to pull the coat close around him. He sat like that a long moment, then abruptly got up and looked at Brandon.

'I guess I'd better get back. Lord knows what's waiting for me.'

They went out together, tromped to the barn where Brandy hitched the doctor's buggy to his horse, handed the lines to the doctor and stood in the gloom of predawn in the maw of the barn, feeling the thoughtful glance of the medical man fully on him.

'Thanks, Brandy.' He juggled the lines a little. 'I hate to say it, boy, but you're making a war out of this.'

'I'm not making it, Doc. She put up the fence. She's got to make it stick. You know how those things work, here.'

'I know something else, too, Brandy. The cowmen'll take this damned hard.'

Brandy lifted one soggy boot and put it on the little iron step of the buggy. 'Listen, Doc, she made the fence, I didn't. She put a lot of money into it. Her idea behind it was good, but without someone to back her up the damned thing wouldn't be left up twenty-four hours.'

'And that someone is you, eh?'

'Who else? Her brother – even if he could – is knocked out.'

'Well, I guess it's hopeless then, isn't it?'

'Not if the cowmen'll leave her fence alone, it isn't.'

The doctor lifted the lines, clucked at his horse. 'That's the same thing, Brandy. Hopeless.'

Brandon stood in the doorway of the barn watching the doctor's rig skid and rock through the mud puddles, lift gently when it came to the first landswell, then top a flat, dark ridge, hang there a second and drop from sight.

Daylight was trying to drive its wedge of light through the overcast. A long way off some big hills looked like cardboard imitations, all gray-black, starkly outlined and brooding, their ridges whip-sawed with patches of timber.

Even if he hadn't been up all night, didn't have a leaden feeling in his belly, the grayness of the world would have depressed him. He thought of the bunkhouse, its carbolic smell, the blank faces, smoke, expressionless eyes, and wished he had a cigarette. The door of the house swung open and a patch of light fell outward, slewed across the rain puddles. He saw her outline.

'Brandy?'

'Yes'm.'

He started across the yard. Was half-way across it before he sensed something in the heavy atmosphere, stopped and threw up his head. Horses coming. Riders. A quick-running chill held him momentarily. He turned into the north, peering. The sound reached ahead of the figures, but he was still standing there when he saw them, little fading raindrops darkening the yoke of his shirt. He couldn't count them as they topped the ridge the doctor had recently gone over, because they didn't pause, but he saw enough. It was a large body of riders coming slowly, purposefully, toward the ranch. Their slickers shone wet-shiny in the gray light of dawn.

He sprinted toward the bunkhouse, entered softly and jerked his head at the men lying on their bunks, talking drowsily. 'Posse or something coming. About fifteen or so horsemen. Get dressed and armed and go to the barn. Take your carbines. Watch the house, I'll be over there.' He backed out of the room, closed the door with a rapid glance at Cal, whose eyes were closed, lips and cheeks blue looking.

Marti had pushed the doughnut bowl closer to where he'd sat before. She had also refilled his cup with coffee. There was a rich aroma of frying meat in the warm room when he entered, closed the door and looked over at her. She came around with the same set expression, looked at him and her eyes widened. Almost too softly she said:

'What is it, Brandy? Why are you looking that way? What's wrong?'

'There's a band of riders coming. I – don't like the looks of it.' He strained to hear. No sounds came through the walls. 'Listen, Marti–'

'No, *you* listen. Oh, Brandy – we can't *do* this. A man's been killed. We can't go on with it. There'll be more killings.'

'PARKER!'

Her face blanched. 'Who was that?'

He shook his head, felt for the door latch

181

behind him. 'It's our visitors, I reckon. You bolt this door behind me, Marti.'

'No!' She was holding one wrist with a white-knuckled hand. 'You can't go out there, Brandy—'

'Don't get hysterical, Marti. Don't make it any worse. I can't fight for you and against you both. Do as I say...'

'PARKER! COME OUT OF THERE!'

'Lock the door after me and whatever happens stay inside. Don't *do* that,' he said huskily, when her eyes misted, her mouth quivered. 'The boys are over in the barn watching. Nothing's going to happen.'

He lifted the latch, swung through the smidgin of opening and closed it behind him.

He had been wrong, there weren't fifteen of them, there were twelve, but he had no doubts about that, either. They'd left a few off as they'd ridden on in. The others would be squatting in the gray light around the buildings. Out on the range somewhere. Holding their reins in one hand, carbines in the other, waiting.

Jared Hoxey's round, weathered face was far beneath a big black hat, shadowed and watchful looking. The Spanners were on either side of him. Wagonwheel riders sat the horses in the background. He recognized the big one named Sims he'd pulled Arty Fortin out from under. Two of the Turlock boys were in the band. Bow riders, too, some he knew, some of the faces were too hidden under hats or updrawn coat collars, slickers. Jared Hoxey's mouth moved just enough to let words out, the rest of his face was like ruddy iron.

'You're going back to town with us, Brandy. There's a warrant out for you for murder.'

'Who did I murder?' He stood on the veranda, his right arm away from the gun at his hip.

'Sam Morton – and you know it. Go get your horse.' Hoxey's little eyes flickered over the house. 'Don't make a break, Brandy. You got less chance than a Chinaman in hell.' Hoxey's head rocked sideways brusquely. 'Go fetch your horse.'

Brandon remained motionless. 'When a lawman comes for me with a warrant I'll come in. When you fellers come, you're wasting your time.'

Fat Spanner swung out of his saddle and the leather creaked. No one spoke. Hoxey's little eyes never left Brandon's face. Spanner's brothers eased down, too. The three of them looked squatty and thick under their slickers, ranged side by side, Fat the widest and shortest. Brandon's mouth tightened. It had all been planned ahead, he saw that. If Hoxey couldn't talk him into going along the Spanners would beat him into going along. He looked down at them, backgrounded as they were by the solid wedge of horsemen, all like statues.

'Don't try it, boys. There're guns on you from the barn over there.'

Hoxey spoke again. 'I don't think you'll do that, Brandy.' He said it slowly. 'I don't think you'll turn this ranch into a graveyard. We know how many men you got. That's why we brung this many. Someone's going to get hurt, now, you mark my word. We come out here to get you, to take you back to town and lock you up, and we're going to do it one way or another.'

'Take me to town?' Brandon said. 'Take me to the nearest tree, Jared. If you're using that "town" talk for my benefit save your breath. I've known you all my life, Jared. What I don't know I've heard from the oldtimers. You've used hangrope justice before. Well – not this time you don't, and if you're hell bent on trying it come ahead – you and Fat – but by God I know *you* won't ride out of the yard when it's over, Jared. Not you.'

Hoxey's cheek twitched. 'Most men you could have in that barn's five. We got twice that many right here. There's more we didn't bring in with us. You comin' Brandy? It's up to you. Come along peaceful or tied over a horse – you don't kill a man like Sam Morton and get off scot-free.'

Brandon leaned against a porch upright. He didn't answer. Hoxey's cheek twitched again. Softly he said, 'Go get him, Fat.'

Fat Spanner started through the mud. Brandon could hear the sucking sounds as he pulled his booted feet out of the mud. Fat's brothers Jim and Ed slogged along on either side of the squatty man. When they were at the bottom of the steps Brandon's thoughts crystallized, meshed with the speed of light behind his eyes. If he fought them, he had no doubt in the world that Hoxey meant exactly what he had said. There would be a knockdown drag-out battle in the yard. The cowmen had come there for just exactly that. If he went with them – he knew what they intended to do. He stiffened against the upright.

'Hold it, Fat.'

The Spanners stopped. Fat had his arm out to keep his brother Ed back. Ed, younger, dull-witted, bull-like, obeyed only one man on earth; Fat.

'You won't do it, Fat. Not all three of you won't.'

Fat let his arm drop. Up until now he hadn't spoken a word to anyone since riding into the Grant ranch yard. He lifted one leg and set the foot down solidly on the next step. 'We'll do it. Came here to do it.' He moved up another step, looked up at Brandon and closed his mouth tightly, the ripple of jaw muscles flickering in the dingy light.

'You're too close, Fat. I can't miss.'

Fat stopped again, looking up, his brothers, behind him paused. There was a moment of terrible silence – then a baby's fretful cry broke it. The sound rose and fell with gasping interludes. A sick-husky voice tried to stop the crying and Brandon's high shoulders went lower, drooped.

'Hold it. Fat … I'll come along.'

Jared Hoxey's breath rattled in the stillness that followed Brandon's words. 'Get your horse, Brandy. Tell your men not to start anything. We'll kill that kid – you know that, don't you?'

Fat Spanner, the bulky shapes of his brothers behind him, stood uncertainly on the steps looking up at the tall man on the porch.

Brandon moved. 'I'll get the horse…'

He went down the steps. Fat Spanner moved, swayingly when Brandon was close, lifted his gun from its holster and held it lightly in his hand. Brandon went on past, down into the muddy wash of the yard, turned right past the body of horsemen who watched in stony silence, trudged toward the barn.

Cal was in the forefront of the clutch of men when Brandon entered the barn. He was holding a double-barrelled shotgun with both hands. 'Brandon – we can cut 'em down like hay, boy.'

The gloom of dawn was deeper, solider,

inside the barn. Emory had his ivory-butted pistol in his fist, his dark eyes like wet obsidian, his teeth rusty-white. 'Odds're in our favor,' he said as Brandon stopped. 'We've got the barn – they're in the open.'

'You couldn't get them all, fellers. There're more beyond the ranch somewhere. I know those men.'

'We could run 'em–'

'No you couldn't. Listen – you might get five or six of them. The rest would fan out, hide. They'd fire the house. I know how they'd work.'

'The house?' Cal said, comprehending slowly.

'Yeah. They'd burn it. You know what'd happen to Milt and the baby?' He nodded at Emory. 'Get my grulla horse, will you?'

Emory straightened up slowly, holstered his gun and turned away. Brandon's gaze fell on some carefully stored, laboriously made lengths of wooden water pipe. These things were simply hollowed out saplings, the core burnt with hot rods. Rawhide was wrapped around the joints and allowed to shrink-dry. Every ranch with water in its houses had water pipes like those. The men were talking to him, he scarcely heard them.

'Cal, cut off a couple of lengths of water pipe for me. Make 'em about a foot long. Here, you fellers, break your bullets loose from the tips and pour the powder into the pipes Cal's getting. Plug both ends when the things're full. Stick a few whole bullets inside, too. You've got to work fast.'

Emory came up out of the bowels of the barn with the grulla horse. Brandon turned, held out his hand for the lead-rope. 'Get my saddle-gear, Emory. Bring it right up here in the doorway. No hurry.'

Emory looked puzzled. Cal was hacking away at the hollowed saplings. Men were breaking cartridges. They all understood what Brandon wanted done. None knew why and Brandon himself wasn't sure; a desperate moment prompted desperate measures.

'Want me to saddle him up?'

'I'll do it.'

He did, slowly, keeping an eye on the cowmen, moving lethargically, heavily, until Cal handed him the two plugged lengths of pipe with sweat from his labours standing out like transparent wax on his face.

Brandon went around on the off-side of the grulla, used his pocketknife to gouge some of the rag plugging loose, let the dark, gray-black grains of gunpowder roll down into the ragging, worked it well in with his fingers, his heart beating harshly, then he shoved both lengths of pipe inside his shirt, motioned toward Cal's slicker, which was handed him. He donned it, turned the horse once, stepped up and lifted the reins.

'When we're gone, you fellers fan it for

town. Go roundabout so you're not seen. Go fast or I'm a goner. Fetch back the law and all the help you can get. Tell Marti not to worry – and if anything goes wrong tell her good-bye…'

He rode toward the cowmen. They didn't wait for him to get close, impatience was stamped on every face among them. They seemed to just naturally envelope him, sweep him northward out of the yard as they rode. The only sound was horses' hooves in the mud, a sucking, sloppy sound. That and saddle-leather, jingle of rein-chains, spur rowels.

Jared Hoxey reined back until he was beside Brandon. His hat still shadowed his face, but where his hands had been bare before they were now gloved. The danger was past; Hoxey no longer felt he might need his fingers free to curl around a gun-butt.

'I'm sorry about this, Brandy,' he said it tonelessly, like he really was sorry. 'I'm disappointed in you, too. I knew your paw real well. Even knew the Old Gent a little. They were cowmen.'

Brandon gazed detachedly at the weathered, iron-hard profile. What Hoxey said was so. He wasn't a bad man; few men were. Killing like this, hanging a man, was a means of holding a country subjugated to cow law; to cowmen it had to be done every once in a while. They didn't like to do it;

they simply knew that they had to do it. The gray overcast made faces old, lined, grim-visaged lips blue and downward looking, eyes lusterless.

'…No right to try to change a country that's been like it always since before you was born. I got to stop talking, Brandy…'

They plodded through the murky country-side like specters and the cowed look to everything, even the horses they rode, head down, and the sound of the soggy earth underfoot found a gray response in Brandon's spirit. Once he lifted his head and looked eastward. There was nothing but the ageless landscape there. Southward, too, lay a pall of stillness, of lead-like shimmerings from hundreds of little puddles. He thought back to the ranch. Maybe the riders would get to Charley in time, but if his reckonings were right Charley and half the townsmen were already ahorseback, splattering them-selves with blobs of mud, wrathful-eyed searching. And Marti…

'Yonder's a tree,' Ed Spanner said in his thick, dull-witted way. Another rider blew his nose with his fingers, hawked and spat. Fat Spanner was making a cigarette, head tilted, hatbrim low over his face, reins swinging from side to side as his horse kept pace with those around him.

'I said there's a tree, yonder, you fellers.'

'Shut up, Ed, dammit.' Fat flicked a match,

lit up and thumbed the match in an arc. He never once looked around at Brandon.

A Wagonwheel man swore fitfully at his horse when the animal put its ears back and tried to bite the strange horse beside it. Far enough, Brandon thought. Far enough from the ranch to hold 'em a while – if it works.

He worried one hand under Cal's slicker, groped for the opening in his shirt, fondled the two warm, hollowed saplings. Felt for the powder-saturated fuses, pinched them and withdrew his fingers, looked at them and saw the little gray-black flecks of powder. He wiped them off on the slicker and spoke.

'Who's got the makings?'

A Bow cowboy beside him held out a sack. He looped his reins and worried up a cigarette, lit it with a match from the same hand and handed the tobacco back. Rode another hundred yards then very casually reached inside his shirt, withdrew one of the pipes, held the rag-end to his cigarette and with a grunt and a mighty heave threw the thing as far outward as he could. It exploded almost before it touched the ground. The noise was deafening. Two horses bawled and went to bucking, heads bogged, stiff-legged. Both unseated their startled riders.

Riders were spun in every direction. Some called out profanely, others fought their mounts to a standstill. All were thrown into a welter of confused men and animals. Jared

Hoxey's hat lay in the mud, trampled, his scant hair askew.

'What?'

Brandon quieted the grulla, reined up and held both hands higher than his saddlehorn. Hoxey was staring at him. Fat Spanner, white-faced, had his gun out and cocked, and was urging his snorting horse closer.

'What was that, Brandon?'

'A bomb, Fat. Look.' He withdrew the second one, held it close to the fragment of brown-paper cigarette between his lips. 'If I touch it to the cigarette it goes off.'

'Don't!'

Their eyes held. 'Why not?' Brandon said. 'What's the difference *how* a man dies when his time comes?'

'Don't – you damned fool. I'll gut-shoot you.'

'Go ahead.' Brandon could smell the acrid odor of the powder so close to his face. 'Like I said – what's the difference how it happens? Gun, rope, bomb. Go ahead, Fat, pull the trigger.'

'Hold it, Fat,' Jared Hoxey said in a forced calm way, coming closer. 'Brandy, throw that thing down. No – wait; I'll take it.'

Brandon's eyes were smarting from the unaccustomed smoke. 'If you take it, Jared, it'll be to hell with you. Get away, man, I'm not fooling.'

Fat's gun barrel drooped. Hoxey reined up

short. His hair standing up all awry gave him an elfin appearance. 'Brandy–'

'Shut up, Jared. You fellers – I'll give you a twenty second start.'

'Shoot him in the back,' Ed Spanner interrupted thickly, his eyes wide with hate and terror both. 'I can–'

'Damn you, Ed,' his brother said. 'Don't make a move. Shut up now.'

'Twenty seconds, fellers, then anyone who's close by goes to hell with me.'

Several of the cowboys unconsciously lifted their rein hands. 'Wait,' Jared began. Brandon started to count, the words came spaced, a little deflected by the closeness of the bomb to his cigarette. '...seven, eight, nine, ten – Fat, you and Jared, by God I'm not kidding – eleven, twelve–'

'We'll kill you, Brandy.'

'...thirteen, fourteen – you won't have to, this thing will – sixteen–'

'You skipped fifteen – Kee-rist! Run fer it, boys.'

Jared shouted at them. Fat started to yell, too, but the words died on his lips. Still holding his gun he had to swerve his horse as his brother Jim went careening frantically by. Ed caught in the same grip of panic, let out a slobbering wail and almost lifted his mount off the ground with his hooks. The horse lashed his tail and bolted. That was when Fat and Jared both raised their guns.

It was also the desperate second when Brandon touched the rag to the end of his cigarette and threw it straight at the only two men whose nerve had matched his own.

Hoxey's horse swerved first. He was spurring, urging his beast to flight before the bomb was close. Fat, in the face of Hoxey's terror and the uncertainty of his own destruction, caved. He took a shot, but it was far high. The bomb fell where they had been with mud cascading all around it from furiously fleeing riders.

Brandon raked the grulla once, that was all it took. The animal leapt out with an angry baring of its teeth, ran belly-down, ears back and furious eyes alight. Threw up big hunks of slippery mud and never once slackened speed.

When the bomb went off the grulla sucked his hind-end under him like he'd been hit across the rump with a chain, crossed leads in mid-stride and ran for all he was worth. Brandon made no attempt to use the reins. They were going too fast. The ground underfoot was too slippery, and the animal was panicked. He felt Cal's slicker straining across his shoulders and groped backwards to pull it down. It was trailing straight out behind him. He tucked enough of it under him to hold it down, then twisted for a look. Riders were scattered out on both sides of him and far behind as well. Other horsemen were loping out of the distance toward the scene of disturbance. He guessed them to be the men Jared and Fat had stationed around the ranch out on the range. Off on his left a carbine cut loose. Almost before he looked he was tugging gently lightward on his reins. The grulla responded, came around in a big half circle. The cowboy was riding toward him from a brush-draw ahead and to his left. Evidently he'd been one of those out-riders, for his horse seemed perfectly under control.

Brandon swung still farther southward, riding like the wind, and a mile later he eased the grulla more west than south. It was a fast, wild ride. A ragged line of hard-riding horsemen were thundering through the mud after him, but he had too good a start to fear even their carbine fire.

The race continued in grim silence except for the sounds of the horses laboring through the soggy mud, their breath steaming into the cool stillness, until Brandon saw the windmill, the top of the Grant ranch's old log barn, lift reluctantly ahead of the drop-off of the range ahead. He knew he was safe; at least for a while.

His horse skidded, stumbled and almost fell when he yanked him into a slide before the house, slammed down into the mud and ran wetly toward the veranda. The animal shook his head and turning, trailed the reins to one side so as not to step on them and started across the yard toward the barn. Brandon hit the door with his fist, straining for the first signs of the pursuit. Marti opened it with a big pistol in her hand, her face white and red-eyed looking.

'Brandy!'

He reached for the pistol. Its butt felt good against the palm of his hand. 'Close the door!' Movement out of the corner of his eye brought his head up. 'Milt!'

The boy had a carbine in his bony hands, the wild look in his eyes. 'They're comin', Brandon?'

'Yeah. Be here in a few minutes. I ran away from them.'

'Where're the riders?'

'I sent them after help before I left.'

The ashen face with its two high splotches of color, high, under each shining eye, looked defiant. 'I saw 'em ride out of the yard. We've got this one to ourselves, then, I guess.'

'Milt: if you want to help, fine, but do it lyin' on the couch over there by the window or in your room, lyin' down. You're not in shape–'

'You wouldn't have thought so if you'd seen me when you were talking to them on the porch, Brandy. I had the shotgun on 'em. It'd've been like shooting fish in a rainbarrel!'

'All right,' Brandon said. 'But do it lyin' down, Milt, will you?'

A ghostly flicker of a grin hovered over the boy's mouth. 'Sure,' he said. 'You're the boss.' He shuffled painfully toward a leather sofa over against the wall, behind which were two windows that looked out onto the veranda and the yard beyond.

Brandon turned to Marti. 'Got any more bullets for this?'

She nodded without speaking, went to a shelf, stood on tiptoes and felt around above her head. He could see the box she was feeling for, crossed the room and reached for it over her head. She came back down on her heels, turned. He had the box. It felt full. Their eyes met. The funny feeling returned with a rush. She looked helpless, really lost and helpless, for the first time since he'd met her. Little, lost, helpless, but sturdy, a scale-model of something coarser, fine-drawn and tiny and...

'Petite, Marti – that's that word I've been trying to remember. Petite.' It elated him, pushed out and back his other anxieties. 'Petite.'

'Kiss me, Brandy,' she said it almost forlornly, putting her head back, rocking forward on her tiptoes again.

He kissed her. Used both arms to engulf her; smelled the golden fragrance of her hair. Felt the frightened tremor pass over her.

'I'd better say it, Brandy. I don't think you ever will and I've got an awful feeling about this – all this – fighting and killing... Brandy, I love you.'

He just held her, didn't move nor speak nor look down at her. His head was bursting with a giddiness he'd never known before. Love? He loved her. Good God Almighty – he'd loved her that day she'd smiled her guileless smile and handed him the reins to her sorrel mare: had come back later and handed him something that turned out to be a baby. Loved her right then, plumb out of the blue, like something that happened to a man and he couldn't stop it any more than he could fly.

Her fingers worked up behind his neck, the nails worried his flesh, made goose-bumps jump out all over him and his stomach go flat and deflated-feeling. His knees floated in pools of liquid and his breath sounded like a horseshoe-rasp sliding over a jagged edge of glass.

'I love you, Marti. But I've got to think about?'

'Why? Am I too little for you – or something?'

He tried to pull back and look at her, but she wouldn't let him... She held on tightly. 'What's that got to do with it – your size?'

'Well – *I* don't know, Brandy – but you've – well – just once, the night of the dance; that's the only time you ever acted like you loved me. I'm not ugly, Brandy – am I?–

Then it had to be something else. Too little for a Western man, maybe – or because of the baby – or maybe Milt–'

'That don't – doesn't – make sense, Marti. Size, the baby, Milt – none of it's got anything to do with loving you. It's just that I'm not sure what love *is*– I–'

'Can't you feel I can. I've felt it since that day in the saloon, Brandy. It kept getting worse, too, waiting for you to say something.' She snuggled closer, worried her face into his chest. 'I guess it's just about worse than being shot, sometimes, only you wouldn't know, Brandy. I *thought* you did. I thought you loved me. Then I didn't know. Then I was afraid you didn't and never would. All those times you could've said something, Brandy – like yesterday in the blacksmith's shop. And when the others go outside to smoke and you – don't smoke – and could've stayed in the kitchen with me.'

'Well gosh. Marti–'

She closed her fingers on his shoulders. The nails bit through his flesh, hurt, made fire and fury rage in his blood in a wild breathless way. She shook him.

'What is there to *think* about, Brandy? You do or you don't.'

'Well,' he was perspiring like a horse, could feel the blood beating, wave after wave, into his face. 'If wanting you is love, thinking about you is love, seeing you as clear as a picture is love – then I've got it. I had to figure it out – I haven't done this much before, Marti. It's sort of scairy.'

'And fear, Brandy. Fear's love, too, and I'm scairt to death right now. Right this instant.' She drew in a big, wavering breath and let it out, put both palms against his chest and pushed.

They looked at one another in a depth of solemnity then she colored and half turned aside.

'Marti, I love you. I want to marry you. Will you?'

'Yes.'

A whistling breath came from the couch over by the window. They both swung around. Milt, mouth agape, carbine dangling from one hand, was staring, stunned and staring and absolutely wordless. Marti's face flamed. Brandy looked to be in shock or fever or both.

Chapter Seven

Milt looked like he'd been gut-kicked by a mule. Too astounded to move. Into the stillness came the sound of horsemen. It jarred Brandon back to reality. Moving swiftly, he crossed the room in two strides, bent and peered out the window. A kaleidoscope of events compressed into seconds held him rooted. The horsemen were strung out, but a tall, leggy gray with dapples down his legs was throwing up his head under a tugged back rein. The rider sat easy, hand-gun up, twisted a little in the saddle to see the house, when a carbine exploded and the horse gave a violent leap, lit wide-legged, head down and bucking, mane and tail swirling wildly. The rider wasn't set, he fought for his balance, lost it and went off sideways, pinwheeling into the mud. Brandon was stunned. Milt brushed his shoulder.

'Who the hell fired?'

Brandon didn't answer right away. The other horsemen were fanning it hard, throwing up great gobs of mud in their eagerness to get clear of the yard. Over the scene hung a sow-belly sky, putrid white and pregnant looking, swollen, grayish.

'Somebody's in the bunkhouse,' Brandon finally said. 'One of the riders must have stayed back – thank the Lord.'

Outside, a man's high, strong voice called out for the riders to take cover. Brandon tilted his pistol barrel, struck lightly at the window glass, broke it, drew down on the man in the mud and called out.

'Drop it, mister!'

The dripping hulk turned, raised its head. Ed Spanner. Brandon smiled to himself thinly. 'Drop it, Ed, or you'll stay there with it.' Ed understood. His mouth was working over incoherent words. He held his arm out and dropped the pistol. Mud was caked over him, all but the frightened little eyes. 'Now – walk over to the bunkhouse. The boys over there'll take care of you.' Spanner slogged his way across the yard. It was deathly still. Brandon turned toward Marti. 'Keep a watch out back, will you, Marti? Thanks to the rain they can't burn us out of here from long-range, but they might if they got up close.'

She moved off and two gunshots blasted the silence. In the back of the house Brandon heard the baby give a frightened, loud bellow. His mouth twitched.

Milt raised the carbine laboriously, lay it over the sill and leaned low. 'There's one slipping behind the barn. I'll fix his wagon for him.'

Brandon laid his free hand on the carbine barrel. 'Don't shoot to kill, Milt.'

The boy crooked his head, looked up with perplexed, half-angry eyes. 'Why not, for gosh sakes, they tried to kill me, didn't they? They're trying to kill us all now, aren't they?'

Brandon moved off to one side of the window. 'Milt, when this is over you won't want folks to point you out as a killer. Keep 'em away is all. Don't try to kill them. This won't last long.'

Milton's face looked defiant. 'Won't last

long? Are you crazy? There's a whole slug of them and one of us in the bunkhouse, you and me here – it won't last long if we *don't* shoot to kill, Brandy.'

Brandon shook his head at the youth. 'Do like I say, Milt, or I'll take that gun away from you.'

Milt's nostrils quivered, his mouth drew inward. Got flat looking. Brandon was watching him. He opened his mouth to say something when Marti came back into the room, crossed over to them, saw Milt's hard expression and looked quickly at Brandon.

'What's the matter?'

'There's help coming, I think, and I don't want Milt to kill anyone. Just shoot close enough to keep them away, is all.'

Marti went closer to Milt. But for Brandon's restraining arm she would have exposed herself at the window. 'Milt – you do what Brandy says, he *knows!*'

Milton's eyes wavered under the quick lash of his sister's anger. 'I think it's crazy, Marti. Here we are, fighting for–'

'You do what he says!'

Milt swallowed, looked out into the lowering day and rippled his jaw muscles. 'All *right;* but if they come up around the house I won't promise you a thing – you or him.' He swung his thin back on them both in high dudgeon and leant over the carbine again.

'Any of them around in back, Marti?'

'Not that I saw. The baby's awake, Brandy, I'll have to stay with him. But I'll call you if I see anything.'

'Sure,' Brandy said, smiling a little. 'Be careful, Marti.'

'*You* be careful.' She had a strained, shaken look.

Milt said, without looking around: 'Now, don't start *that* again. We got a war on our hands.'

Marti turned, made a cautious circuit of the room and left them. Brandon watched her as long as he could see her, then swung his gaze to the yard. 'It's pretty quiet out there, Milt.'

'Yeah. They might be–'

'PARKER! HEY, BRANDY PARKER!'

Milt started at the strength of the bellow. 'Who's that?' he said.

'Sounds like Fat Spanner.' He poked his head closer to the window and answered the call. 'What do you want?'

'COME OUT, BRANDY. YOU KNOW WHAT'LL HAPPEN IF YOU DON'T. COME OUT NOW – UNARMED – OR WE'LL RUSH THE PLACE!'

Milt raised up to answer, but Brandon put his hand on the boy's neck, and squeezed hard. 'I'll handle this, you just watch that bunkhouse. Unless I'm way off, Cal's the only one in there and he's too weak to help much. If they rush him he's a goner. Watch

204

the bunkhouse, Milt.'

'ANSWER UP, BRANDY. ARE YOU COMIN' OR AIN'T YOU?'

'Fat,' Brandon shouted, 'you've made a lot of mistakes in your life, but rushing this house'll be the biggest mistake and the last one too – I'm not coming out.'

From over by the barn a pistol shot slammed into the day. Brandon and Milt both flinched when the slug grooved the front of the house with a tearing sound. Milt swiveled his gun a little and fired. Two more shots came right back, one from a carbine, then Marti called out and Brandon whirled with a curse, said, 'Watch 'em, Milt,' and hurried through the house until he found her. She was holding the baby and sitting behind a thick walnut dresser as white as a ghost, blue eyes wide, with dark shadows moving in their depths.

'There are four men in the barn, Brandy. I saw them run in.'

He went to the side window, saw nothing and waited. On the far side of the house a shot sounded, glass broke. Marti started in her chair. Brandon crossed swiftly to her side, put a hand on her shoulder and pressed downward.

'Stay right where you are, honey. That was in the kitchen. I'll go out there with Milt. Don't move, you've got the best spot in the house.'

Back in the kitchen Milt threw him a questioning look. He knelt by the boy and raked the muddy yard, spoke while his head was moving. 'She saw four of them run into the barn. Keep an eye on the place,' he pushed his gun through the window frame and dumped a shot into the maw of the barn, 'like that. There's no rear door. They won't fire the place if they aren't sure they can get out again.'

Milt said, 'Oh,' ducked his head and fired the carbine. The slug struck something solid, ricocheted off into the overhead with a spine-tingling whine. Three tongues of flame spat back spitefully and Brandon watched Milt slam two fast ones into the mud just over the sill of the barn. He smiled.

'That's it, Milt. Scare 'em but don't kill 'em.'

The battle never raged, instead it was a grim siege. The cowmen were baffled in their intention to burn the Grant ranch out by the rain and the promise of more moisture that hung heavy in the air. They tried to maneuver their way close enough to the house to rush it, but this was obviously out of the question at the moment. With a pistol and a carbine waiting, no one in their right mind would try to storm across the slippery yard and up to the house.

'Brandy: why doesn't that feller in the bunkhouse open up again?'

'My guess is that he couldn't if he wanted to. If that's Cal he's in pretty bad shape for firing even that once. With Ed Spanner to watch he's out of it.' Brandon stared at the square little building. 'I'm sure glad it's water-soaked, Milt. If they set it afire Cal'd get cooked.'

'You said we wouldn't have long to hold 'em off – why?'

Brandon didn't get a chance to answer. Someone let out a cry and several others took it up. A ragged fusillade of gunfire erupted from several directions at once. Out of the dismal day came a loud, deep yell, then the thunder of running horses. Brandon dropped to one knee, hardly breathing. Milt's tousled head was low over the carbine. His lips were moving in a faint, nervous way.

A rash of gunshots sounded somewhere a long way off. Marti came into the room hugging the baby to her, her hair awry, hugging the nape of her neck in curling waviness.

'Brandy! There was an army of them on the hill behind the house just now. I saw them.'

'How many?'

She shook her head in a frantic, despairing way. 'I don't know. It looked like an army, really. Fifty anyway. Oh, *Brandy!*'

He stood up quickly, crossed to her side. 'Make us some coffee, Marti, I think our war's just about won!'

She looked blankly at him. 'Won? Didn't you hear me? *I saw at least fifty riders up on the hill behind the house!*'

Milt's voice lashed the air. 'Brandy! They're coming…!' Milt levered and fired.

Brandon spun away from Marti. Six men were coming toward the house from the direction of the barn. They were pumping lead from hand-guns, crouched, slipping, slogging through the mud. Brandon saw the course of Milt's barrel. He touched the youth. 'Lower, Milt, lower. At their legs.'

Milt's reply was lost in the crashing tumult of gunfire. Brandon knelt beside the couch, struck another pane of glass with his tilted-back barrel, thumbed off a shot, saw the mud fly, thumbed off a second one and drew back his pistol, squatted and began to re-load, watching the advancing men waver, their guns rocking back each time they fired. The house echoed with dull sounds where slugs struck it. A pane blew apart over Milt's head. He had presence enough of mind to duck low, throw one arm over his head. Marti made a high, bleating sound. Brandon grabbed for her, jerked her roughly back, then a roar like the bellow of an enraged bull broke over the gunfire and a blast of shots splattered the six advancing riders with mud. They broke, turned and fled back toward the mud. Milt raised his head. A thin spindrift of blood trickled lazily down his forehead.

White and furious he crouched over his carbine, tracked one fleeing man and fired. The rider let out a scream and fell flopping in the dirt, writhed and rolled, got to his feet and shambled draggingly after the others.

'BRANDY! HOLD IT A MINUTE. IT'S ME – CHARLEY! YOU HEAR ME?'

Brandon punched in his last shell, snapped the ejection gate closed and dropped the pistol into his holster. 'Yeah, I heard you, Charley. What kept you?'

'WE'RE BRINGIN' THEM INTO THE YARD, BRANDY. DON'T SHOOT!'

'We won't. Come on.'

Marti put a hand slowly up and brushed her hair back. 'Is it really him? Brandy...?'

'It's him all right, I'd know that bellow anywhere.'

Milt sat up shakily, fingering the thin gash on his forehead. He was looking up at Brandon. 'That's what you mean. I understand now. You sent the riders for him.'

'Well – not just for him, exactly. I worked a little shenanigan, too. We'll see if it worked.'

Marti, hugging the baby, who wasn't especially excited, but who was wide awake and fascinated by his fingers, said: 'I'll make the coffee.'

Brandon smiled at her. There was a core in his throat.

Milt's grunt brought his attention back to the yard through the shattered window.

'Look at 'em, Brandy. Hell; there must be twenty of them.'

Brandon looked. They were afoot, jostling one another through the slippery mud, arms over their heads, slickers unbuttoned, flying loosely around their bodies, some hatless. He recognized Jim Spanner first, then one of the Turlock boys, and along toward the drag, Jared Hoxey, his squat, bull-like figure looking shorter, broader, beside the tall riders who slogged along around him.

He wasn't conscious of Marti until she said, 'Look,' at his elbow, and pointed to the barn and corral area. Men on horseback were herding other men, afoot, out of the barn, around the corrals, at gun-point. 'Who are they all, Brandy? Did Charley get a posse?'

'Sort of. I think the posse got him, more than he got them.'

She looked up but he didn't turn. The riders came behind the cowmen, a band of them at least twenty-five strong. More riders came in from other directions around the ranch. They seemed to be riding out of the dismal weather itself, like mounted phantoms, dim shapes that took on perspective, depth, the closer they got. Guns flashed with dull, sodden reflection. Guns and wet slickers and pulled-down hats that hid faces of men.

Brandon recognized Charley Belton first, then he saw a man he knew from his last visit to Fallbrook, then another shape, whose eyes, behind their spectacles, looked large, magnified. Other men, too, from Fort Parker. Charley Belton leaned from his saddle and prodded a man in the back of the neck with his carbine, one-handed. His words were lost to the watchers in the house. Brandon called out to him.

'There's one in the bunkhouse, Charley, it's Ed Spanner.'

Charley straightened, threw a glance toward the house and his teeth flashed in the dark shadow of his face. He turned and spoke. A little squad of horsemen rode toward the bunkhouse. Charley turned back, settled deeper into his saddle, let his shoulders droop and lay his carbine across his lap, put both hands on the horn and called out to Brandy.

'Come on out. I think the fight's all out of them.'

Brandon turned toward the door, collided with Marti. The dazed, terrified look was gone. In its place was something hard to define, a sort of she-wolf cold stare of triumph with just a hint of ruthlessness in it. He bent swiftly, kissed her squarely on the mouth and gently took her by the shoulders, moved her aside.

'Get that coffee hot. General Grant or somebody said an army travels on its stomach. There's a lot of stomachs out there.'

He went out, down the steps and through

the mud. Fat Spanner was squarely in front of him. He stopped, exchanged stares with Fat a second, his mouth curled slightly in a cold grin. 'Fat; I think you've got a wrong idea.' Fat didn't answer. His eyes stayed steady, unblinking. 'Earlier – back there on the steps – you had an idea you could whip me. I don't think you can.'

Charley Belton said: 'Brandy!'

'Wait a second, Charley. This won't take long. How about it, Fat: want to have at it?'

Fat didn't move. His broad shoulders hunched forward just the smallest bit. He dropped his arms to his sides, seemed to be thinking, then he said, 'No, I reckon not, Brandy.'

A man dismounted, walked around the captured cowmen grimly, looking at none of them. 'Brandy.' Brandon turned. It was the sheriff. His face looked drawn and upset. He held out his hand. The badge Brandon had sent Emory to put in Sam Morton's pocket lay in his palm. 'How did this get in Morton's pocket?'

'Why do you want to know?' Brandon said quietly.

The sheriff closed his fist, dropped his arm to his side. 'Because the Fort Parker Town Fathers said I'd made Morton my deputy.' The sheriff motioned at the host of horsemen watching with grim, unrelenting stares. 'They damned near threw me in jail when I got to town. I had a hell of a time convincing them I didn't–'

'You didn't *convince* anybody,' a strong voice said. 'We brought you along in case you wasn't lyin'. All you politicians are liars. I wouldn't believe you nor–'

'Rope it, Arty,' Charley said. Arty Fortin subsided with a growling mutter. Charley was looking straight at Brandon with a quarter-grin, waiting.

Brandon nodded at the sheriff. 'Yes, I had that badge put on Morton. I lifted it from Charley's desk and had it stuck in Sam's pocket. You want to know, sheriff; because I wanted Fort Parker to come out here, not just four or five saloon bums. Charley needed a big posse. I figured, as mad as the City Fathers were over the way you handled that deputy business, that'd be about all they needed to get fighting mad.'

The sheriff gazed balefully at Brandon. After a moment he wagged his head and said, 'Well, by God, you figured it just about right.' He stood in silence until the older man with the spectacles nudged his horse up closer, leaned a little from the saddle and bobbed his head.

'Go on, sheriff, spit the rest of it out.'

'I'm going to,' the sheriff said annoyedly. He held out his fist again. 'Brandy – this is your badge. Will you please take it back? I made a damn fool mistake and I want to apologize to you – to all the folks around Fort Parker. I had no idea these cowmen were up to making a regular issue out of this fence.'

Brandy's smile held when he said, 'Sheriff; do you know what you can do with that badge?'

Charley's voice interrupted. 'Easy, old-timer. It's your job, remember.'

'Not any more, Charley. I'm going to be a rancher – a rider at least. That's how my pa and grandpa got their start. You've got the job. Charley, there isn't a better man in the country for it.'

'Me?' Charley said loudly. 'I'll be damned. Now just a–'

'All right,' Brandon said, his eyes on the tough little man directly behind Charley. 'I'll nominate Arty Fortin there, right behind you, Charley, to fill out my – our – unexpired term. What say, Arty?'

Charley swiveled his head. 'Take it, Arty.'

Fortin's boyish face screwed up. He looked around him. A cowboy laughed in a low, musical way. 'I second that, Brandy. Arty's the man.' The blacksmith was staring at Brandon.

'You won't take it back, Brandy?'

'Never again, I'm sorry.'

'And you, Charley – you won't go on–'

'Not for a million dollars,' Charley said hastily. 'Not for *two* million.'

The blacksmith looked around at the two

other older men beside him. He raised his eyebrows. They both nodded wordlessly. 'All right, Arty – you're the law in town and in the country around here.' He fixed the sheriff with an unfriendly gaze. 'Want to appoint him, sheriff?'

'Glad to – sure.'

Brandon turned a little, found Jared Hoxey's gaze crossing his own. He looked up at the blacksmith. 'How about these rawhiders?'

'They've got a rawhiding coming all right. Think they can run this country liked they have for forty years. Ought to be horsewhipped, the lot of them.'

Charley leaned forward in his saddle. 'What's the damage, Brandy?'

Brandon's gaze held to Hoxey's. He was slow replying. 'Sam Morton dead. Milton Grant wounded – bushwhacked – Cal wounded, one of our riders wounded.' He shrugged, stopped speaking for a moment. 'Was it worth it, Jared?' Hoxey didn't answer, so Brandon answered for him. 'Damages'll come high, Jared – you damned fool. I told Fat those roughshod Colt-law days were over and past.'

'Run 'em in,' someone said – harshly, bitterly. 'Let Arty take 'em in and hold a regular court over 'em – the fools.'

'Yeah.'

'Wait a second,' Brandon said, looking

215

over Jared Hoxey's head at the posse. 'Like the doc says – "let's talk it out." Sure, we can have a court hearing and maybe send a lot of them to prison for a while. Listen – they were going to – well – they didn't come out here to powwow with *me,* exactly but I've got an idea about this.' He dropped his glance to Jared. 'How about it, Jared; the old days gone or aren't they?'

In a low voice Hoxey said, 'They've gone all right, Brandy.' He licked his lips. 'If you'd put gates in that fence I don't think–'

'All right, boys,' Brandy said. 'That's right too. There were two sides right from the start we had a right to the fence. But they had a right to get in and out too, it seems like to me.' He shot a swift look at Charley. 'How about it, Charley? Didn't you and I argue about that once?'

'Well – I don't know as it was an argument exactly, but I've felt right along the out-rangers ought to have a way to get their stuff out, you know that.'

Brandon looked down at Hoxey again. 'Jared – we'll build a gate every mile if you fellers will give your word to keep those gates closed. Will that end it?'

'That'll end it, Brandy.'

The sheriff cleared his throat, opened his mouth to speak. The blacksmith shook his head furiously at him. 'You just listen,' he said. 'We had enough of your goddamned foolishness over here. If you hadn't been so hell-bent on countin' cowman votes in the first place this wouldn't have amounted to much.'

'Well – what about the dead man and the others?'

'What about them,' Brandon shot back. 'Morton got his legally. Jared's got some heavy damages to pay. Listen, you send these fellers away and no one's any better off.'

'There'll be charges…'

'There'll be hell,' Brandon said. 'Cal won't file charges and neither will Milt – I'll promise you that. I'll also promise you that there won't be a single witness to any of this.' He looked around him, saw, for the first time, Emory's ivory-butted gun, his white-shining teeth, saw the other Fallbrook men grouped around Emory. 'How about it? Anyone see any gunfighting or fence cutting or anything at all around here these last few days?' The possemen laughed. Even Fat Spanner smiled. He was looking admiringly at Brandy. Dozens of amused 'No's,' answered him and Brandon looked at Jared Hoxey, 'How about you, Jared? Want to stand the damages or fight it in court?'

'I'll stand the damages, Brandy – and thanks, boy.'

The sheriff was gazing fixedly at Brandon. He finally heaved a big sigh and rammed his fisted hands deep into his pants pockets.

'Well, I guess that's best, anyway, Brandy.'

Brandon nodded. 'Charley: send someone over to see if Cal's all right, will you? He's–'

'He's itchin' for another crack at 'em,' Emory said, grinning fit to bust. 'Said he couldn't think of a worse punishment than to make 'em stick around here and build fence for a month.'

Brandon's feet were cold and clammy in his muddy boots. He said: 'Well – Marti's making coffee, fellers. Suppose we talk the rest of it out over by the veranda. Couple of you boys give her a hand, will you?'

Emory swung down swiftly, still grinning widely. Several others joined him. The men milled uncertainly a minute. Charley got down stiffly and prodded Fat Spanner with his thumb. 'Go on, Fat, get some coffee, but you sure played a smart one when you didn't take him up on that fight. I've seen you both in brawls and Fat – you just aren't in his class, believe me.'

Fat looked at Brandon uncertainly. 'Brandy, I'm a horse's rear no question about it.'

'You'd be a hell of a man, Fat, if you weren't, now and then.' He was moving past Spanner, toward Charley, when the crowd broke up, drifted shuffling, uncomfortably, toward the house. Jared Hoxey remained motionless.

'Brandy? I never apologized to a man in

my life. I'm not ashamed to this time. I'm sorry, boy. It was a damn' fool thing to do. I felt it all along, but you know how it was.'

'I know, Jared. I'm sorry, too. Sooner we all forget it the better.'

'Brandy – about the Grant kid getting shot.'

'Yeah, I know. Sam Morton.'

'Yeah.'

'Go get some coffee, Jared.' He waited until the shorter, older man was moving away, then he grinned at Charley. 'Phew, old-timer – that was too damned close. Next time fly, will you?'

'No next time for me, Brandy, I never lost so much sleep or sweat in my life as I have since I relieved you for one day as deputy.'

'Charley – about that feller Fanning.'

'Yeah. What's the story on that beady-eyed little weasel?'

'Scare the devil out of him and run him out of town, before you hand the works over to Arty, will you?'

'Sure, but what'd he do?'

'Somebody trailed Milt the night he got it. The kid didn't tell me this exactly, but he said he heard a horse behind him. I reckon what happened is that Fanning was working for the cow interests. When Milt said he was going for a ride Fanning knew there were fellers out cutting fence, you see, and he slipped away to back up the fence cutters if trouble came.' Brandon shrugged. 'You can guess the rest.'

'Sure, but how'd you know this Fanning was in with the cowmen? You're just guessing there aren't you?'

'Not exactly, I know Fanning cut the fence after he quit the ranch, Charley, it's marked on him. When you go back take a look at his hands. He's got barbed wire cuts and scratches all over them. One thing sure – you don't want to work much with that stuff if you don't want people to know what you're doing. There's no way under the sun to keep from getting branded by it.'

Charley looked surprised. 'Well, I'll be damned,' he said. 'Guess I'd just never make a deputy sheriff anyway, Brandy. I've been around that squirt for a week and never noticed that.'

'Come on, let's get some coffee, Charley, I got another proposition to make to you.'

'Like what? No damned lawing, now, I'm warning you, Brandy.'

'No, not that. You see, Marti said she'd marry me, Charley, and I need someone to keep my knees from buckling, sort of.'

'Oh,' Charley Belton said, and a shadow passed over his eyes, too faint to see in the murky daylight. 'Best man. All right, Brandy, I'll do that for you if you'll return the favor if I ever get that simple minded.'

They smiled at one another, turned and walked slowly over to where men were drinking coffee in an awkward silence, looking at one another somewhat, but mostly just staring at the ground, and Marti was on the veranda, looking out over the heads at them, the shafts of struggling sunlight falling obliquely over her.

The publishers hope that this book has given you enjoyable reading. Large Print Books are especially designed to be as easy to see and hold as possible. If you wish a complete list of our books please ask at your local library or write directly to:

The Golden West Large Print Books
Magna House, Long Preston,
Skipton, North Yorkshire.
BD23 4ND

This Large Print Book, for people
who cannot read normal print,
is published under the auspices of

THE ULVERSCROFT FOUNDATION

... we hope you have enjoyed this book.
Please think for a moment about those
who have worse eyesight than you ...
and are unable to even read or enjoy
Large Print without great difficulty.

You can help them by sending a
donation, large or small, to:

**The Ulverscroft Foundation,
1, The Green, Bradgate Road,
Anstey, Leicestershire, LE7 7FU,
England.**
or request a copy of our brochure for
more details.

The Foundation will use all donations
to assist those people who are visually
impaired and need special attention
with medical research, diagnosis
and treatment.

Thank you very much for your help.